Not In My Wildest Dreams

by Isabelle Peterson

WARNING: EROTIC ROMANCE… This book contains subject material of an adult nature intended for readers of 18 and older, maybe even 21 and older. In these pages you will find graphic language and sexual encounters that some readers might disagree with: regular sex, BDSM, oral, sex toys, and more. You've been warned. Happy reading!

DISCLAIMER: This is a work of fiction. It is not based on my life, nor any person living or dead. Names, characters, places, and events are the creation of the author's imagination and are used fictitiously, and any resemblance is entirely coincidental. Any reference to historical events, real places or real people are used fictitiously. Other names, characters, places, and events are products of the author's imagination, and any resemblance to actual events or persons, living or dead, is purely coincidental.

Cover designed by Kari Ayasha, Cover To Cover Designs
Formatting by Paul Salvette, BB eBooks

Dedication

I dedicate this book to my husband, Marcus. He's the best
part of all the men in my books.
Supportive, generous, loving, exciting, and romantic.

I love you Marc.

Iz

Acknowledgements

Again I sit down to hammer out an acknowledgment section. And there are so many people I have no idea where to start! It's been an impressive 'army' of friends who have helped make Not In My Wildest Dreams *bigger, better, faster and stronger.*

My family, who has been patient and ridiculously supportive and overlooking my mania and listening to me ramble and freak out—Marc, Taylor and Ian—thank you isn't enough.

My friends—Nancy, Marquette, Mary, Brit, and Chris, I believe I owe you a drink!

Alpha, Beta and proof readers – Wow! Your comments, connections, and insight – along with your eagle eyes for typos and such – you are all a blessing. Not one stands ahead of the other, so I am listing you alphabetically: Ana, Brit, Brittany, Courtney, Dottie, Jade, Jennifer, Jessica, Kelley, Kim, Lisa, Raquel, Rebecca, Shannon, Stephanie M., Stephanie S., Terri and Valerie!!!

Thank you to the authors who inspire, support me, advise me, and offer kind words (again, alphabetically): K. Bromberg, Emme Burton, L. Chapman, L.L. Collins, Melissa Collins, Jennifer Anne Davis, K.M. Golland, Sydney Landon, Jodi Ellen Malpas, Raine Miller, N.M. Silber, S.C. Stephens, Skye Turner, and A.L. Zaun.

Thank you to the bloggers who have supported me. So many to mention here, and daily there are more, but here's a short list of those who have been superstars with promoting Ditching the Dream, and I have already been so helpful with Not In My Wildest Dreams: After Dark Divas, Elle's Book Blog, Erotica Book Club, Eye Candy Bookstore, Fictional Boyfriends, For the Love of Books, Hooked on Books, Love Between the Sheets, and Maria's Book Blog.

Thank you to the *thousands* of women (and a few men) who have bought, and read, Ditching the Dream. Your excitement for what was written and what is to come, connections to the characters, and enthusiasm for my writing is what pushed me further into this world of Indie Publishing, and had me once again staring at a cursor on a white screen to put Jack's story into words. You trusted a new author, and I'm so happy you were not disappointed.

Thank you Kari, of Cover to Cover Designs, for your beautiful covers…

And Paul, from BB eBooks Thailand, for the beautiful touches you've put on the Dream Series with the formatting.

As is the nature of the beast—I'm fearful that I've missed someone, somewhere. It'll hit me at 3am some morning and know that I won't be able to sleep.

PROLOGUE

J ack handed his jacket to the flight attendant of the ridiculously expensive private jet and settled into the leather seat. He could have flown commercial, but he wasn't in the mood to be around other people.

"May I get you something to drink, Mr. Stevens?" the cheery attendant asked.

Accepting her interruption as politely as he could muster, Jack glanced at her name tag. "Yes, Katie. Thank you. I'll have a Scotch, please."

"Right away, Mr. Stevens. Macallan 18, correct?" One thing he loved about flying private was the pre-flight questionnaire. That way, you'd get on the plane and not have to explain a thing.

"Thank you." He nodded, distracted in thought.

Moments later Jack was sipping the brown spirits and trying to calm his nerves. *I should be drinking water after soaking my liver like I did these past few days,* he thought. But his heart ached. A chunk had been ripped out leaving a gaping hole that continued to bleed, so he continued to drink.

He thought about the past week. Beth showing up at his home, so sad and quiet…then telling him that she was going back home to her husband… to try and work things out with him. *It's not right,* he thought. *Beth is mine.* He downed the rest of the Scotch and, shifting in his seat, waited for the Captain to announce clearance and takeoff.

Jack's phone buzzed in his pocket, distracting him from his thoughts. It was a text from his secretary and best friend, Becca.

6:39pm
Schedules rearranged. Peter

```
and Terri on next week's shows.
Return flight from Napa to JFK
confirmed for Sunday. Details in
your email, along with Beth's
address in Napa. Best of luck. Go
get your heart back. I look forward
to seeing BOTH of you next week.
```

Taking a deep breath, Jack shut his phone off and put it in his pocket. He closed his eyes to try and get some much needed sleep during the six hour flight to California.

This has to work. It just has to.

CHAPTER 1

Thirty-four years ago... June, 1979.

"*Clean up in aisle seven,*" the speakers in the tiny, rural Colorado grocery store squawked. Angela sat behind the front counter, just ten feet from me, smirking. Was it really necessary for her to use the speakers? No. She was just being a bitch because she was friends with Jenny. Fucking small town. God, it was last summer that Jenny and I had broken up and still, no one would let it rest. Jenny and Suzie were so mad at me that they started calling me 'Jackass Jack'. So what if I wanted to have a threesome with my girlfriend, and her best friend. I was in high school. I'd read about it in *Playboy* and *Penthouse*. It sounded like a good time. C'mon all that soft skin, double the tits, two mouths...

And it's not like I was looking to get married or anything, especially to Jenny. I wanted Suzie, anyway. She had this rack and an ass that you could bounce a quarter off of. It was kinda why I went out with Jenny in the first place; to hang out with Suzie. But learning that Suzie played for the 'other team,' I had to break up with Jenny after she blabbed to all the girls in school. It was too embarrassing. Hell, I was probably never getting married. I didn't want a ball and chain. Why get pinned down to just one flavor for the rest of time? Four of my seven brothers and sisters were already married, while the other three were in serious committed relationships. The life and fun was just sucked right out of them even before they got hitched.

"You hear that, son?" Mr. Thompson called down aisle nine at me. I was stocking the sugar shelves in the baking aisle. "And it's Tuesday. You know what that means."

Yeah, Tuesday meant delivery day. Around four o'clock, the truck would show up, and I'd be lifting and storing fucking heavy boxes for hours afterwards. I was strong enough, but I'd always leave here aching like an old lady, not that I'd admit it out loud.

"Yes, sir, Mr. Tho—" I called over my shoulder, but he was already gone.

God, I hate this job. But I hated working on the ranch more. They didn't need me there anyway. That was clear. My seven brothers and sisters, their husbands and wives and my parents, even though they were in their late 60s, took care of everything from the fields, to the cattle, to the milk. They loved putting me on muck duty. I didn't want to be a fourth generation rancher, but I didn't want to be a small grocery store stock boy either. Honestly, I didn't know what the hell I wanted to do with my life.

I shoved the last of the five-pound bags of sugar back on the shelf and went to get the mop. Aisle seven meant one of two thing: ketchup or pickles.

After cleaning up the red tomatoey mess in aisle seven, I clocked out on my break and headed out back for a smoke. It was pretty warm for the late June afternoon. I leaned on the wall along the side of Thompson Market that faced Davis Street and lit up a Marlboro. I took in the thick smoke and felt myself mellow as I leaned against the peeling painted wall of the building.

I stood a bit straighter when a sweet 'Vette pulled up. Not a new one. A 1966, cherry-red, convertible Corvette. Gorgeous condition for being 15 or so years old. And then there was the sweet thing behind the wheel. Blonde. And stacked. She was no high schooler.

"Do you work here?" she called out.

"Yeah. Who's askin'?" I said back, trying to act cool.

"How old are you?"

Now we're talkin'. "Old enough. What do you have in mind?"

She turned off the ignition, pulled something from the visor, and stepped out of her car. She stood and faced me, her tight top left little to the imagination.

"Do you like living here?" she asked.

Okay, these questions were getting a little weird, even for me. And I had a lot of weird ideas.

She started to walk up to me, and I got to take in the full effect of 'Ms. 'Vette', and I didn't give a shit anymore that she was asking strange questions. I tugged at my jeans to shift the growing beast that was tucked inside a little too tightly now. She had legs that went on for days under a super short skirt that could be left on for what was going through my mind. And those legs were only made hotter by the black stilettos on her feet.

She stopped a couple feet in front of me. She studied my face, then walked to the side of me. I followed her with my head as she chewed on her lower lip.

"Look forward, please," she said.

"Uh, okay," I scoffed. "Mind clueing me in on what you're doin'?"

"I'm looking."

I glanced to the side, and she *was* looking. Up and down. Felt weird to be standing on Davis Street, with a smokin' hot babe checkin' me out, but I couldn't help being totally turned on by it either. I knew I was hot. But when an older chick thinks you're hot, it's a whole new ballgame.

"What are you? Six foot three? Six foot four?" She walked back in front of me and studied me again.

"Somethin' like that," I shrugged.

"Smile."

"What?" I laughed. I was actually starting to get freaked out. She nodded, and a smile slid across her face.

"You might want to take a picture, it lasts longer."

"That's sort of what I'm hoping for." She finished her appraisal of me and leaned against the wall next to me. Taking the cigarette from my hand, she took a drag. She handed it back to me and I almost came in my pants looking at the red lipstick she left on the butt.

"Eighteen?" she asked, letting out a slim stream of smoke.

"Almost nineteen." I replied.

"You going to college in the fall?"

"Going to the community college just north of Boulder, if I can save enough money."

She nodded pensively and handed me a small card. I took it, but didn't look at it. She pulled her shades off and had me pinned with her shocking blue eyes. Extending her right hand toward me, she started, "Penny Paulson. I'm with Ford out of New York."

I laughed a bit, weakly shaking her very soft, delicate hand. "Sorry, hon. Ford is in Detroit. And wouldn't a Corvette break some sort of rules?"

She looked at me for a second, almost confused, then she started to laugh. "No. Good god, you are a country boy, aren't you?"

"I beg your pardon, ma'am?" *Who is she calling a country boy?*

"Ford *Modeling*. Out of *New York City*." She looked at my face for things to register with me, which they didn't. "As in, my company represents models. The people you see in ads." I raised a brow, still not understanding what this had to do with me. "We're going to turn the male modeling world upside down with a new direction. And you have the 'look'."

I was just taking a drag off my cigarette, which turned out to be a bad idea, because I started coughing on the smoke. When I'd regained most of my cool, I coughed. "Come again?"

"Look, it pays well. Granted it's long hours, under hot lights. Clearly you're a hard worker," she said, checking out my phenomenal biceps. "Modeling isn't easy work. You'll earn every dollar. What's your name?"

"Wait, you're serious? You want me to pose all pretty in front of cameras? Wearing fancy clothes and shit."

"I'm saying, if you can take the time off, I'd like to have you come to New York. We'll get some test shots, see what the clients think."

Shit! She's serious.

"Well, you have my card. I'm on my way back to New York today. Call me. What's your name?"

"Uh, okay. It's Jack. Jack Stevens."

She winked and started to strut back to her car. "Talk to you soon, Jack Stevens!" she hollered, slipping behind the wheel and turning over the engine. She turned up the radio, threw the car in reverse, and after making a three-point turn, got herself back onto Main Street.

I looked around me. Not in my wildest dreams could I wrap my head around what just went down. And, fuck me, there were no witnesses to what had just happened. It must have been a figment of my overactive, virile, teenaged imagination. Surely a hot chick, in a bitchin' car, didn't just stop and offer me a job in New York City—to have my picture taken. But looking down into my hands, I was still holding the cigarette butt with her red lipstick in one hand, and her business card in the other.

Penny Paulson

Ford Models, Inc.

(212) 555-FORD

The card looked legit. She looked legit. *Fuck!* This is crazy.

"Stevens! Break is over! Quit bein' such a slacker and get back on the job. You've still got two aisles to straighten and the delivery truck will be here any minute," Mr. Thompson shouted from the doorway.

I looked at the round, red-faced, balding man, and then back at the card in my hand.

"Mr. Thompson. I've wanted to say this for two years now."

He cocked an eyebrow at me, daring me to say whatever it was I had on my mind.

Don't ever dare a Stevens, I thought. "Mr. Thompson. Sir. You know that song that's playin' on the radio by Johnny Paycheck? Well, it's like he said: Take this job and shove it!"

I took one last drag of my cigarette and stomped it out. I untied the apron. I balled it up, threw it toward the door, and walked away.

"Stevens! You walk away now, you won't get your pay for the week!" he shouted. "And don't even think of groveling for this job back tomorrow," he went on. "I'll have a new kid in your place faster than you can say…"

I never heard how he finished the sentence. I didn't care. I laughed all the way to my beat up F-100. I set my prized, red-lipsticked butt in the ashtray and popped Ms. Paulson's business card into the visor.

I twisted the side view mirror to check out my reflection in the metal-framed square. I knew I was good looking. Shit. Even with a nickname like Jackass Jack I still had girls falling for me. I ran my hand through my thick, dark brown hair playing with the waves that drove the chicks crazy. I kept my hair longer, more for the ladies to run their fingers through and grab. I stared at my dark brown eyes. They were so dark that you couldn't even see the pupil. The girls like to say my eyes were like chocolate. I admired my nose. My mother always said I had a noble nose, straight and narrow. I thought my face was long, but had good bone structure. I had a good chin and cheek-bones, I guess.

I ran my hand over my jaw. I didn't need to shave. I still had a baby face without facial hair to speak of, a Stevens family trait. Not very masculine when half the guys I saw were sporting a full mustache, and many had beards to match. But it allowed my good skin to show. I was lucky to have avoided acne, making it through my teen years with only a zit or two, but nothing major.

I smiled, nodded, and jacked up the radio. Donna Summer was belting her hit *Hot Stuff*. *Yes. Yes I am,* I thought to myself and headed home.

Two hours later, I had pulled all of my money out of my bank account that I was saving for college, a rather impressive four-thousand two hundred and eighty dollars, and told my parents I was going to New York. I think they thought I was kidding. Like the time I was going to start my own car fixing business after I was successful at getting my F-100 up and running. Or the time I was going to be a fitness trainer. I dropped the ball on both of those things. Hell, they probably just didn't care. Same for most of my brothers and sisters. Mike gave me a hundred dollars and told me it was for gas, not hookers. Laura, my closest sister, in both age and relationship, tried to stop me. She said that running away from my problems wasn't the answer. Only thing was, I wasn't running away from my problems. I was off to bigger and better things. Good money so I could go to college. Had to be better than stocking shelves for Mr. Thompson. This was fate.

CHAPTER 2

Two and half days of driving and sleeping in my beat up truck, I finally reached New Jersey. I was almost there! I saw a billboard for a hotel comparing their rates to New York City room rates and did some quick math. I'd never been good in school, but $35.00 a night here, or $85.00 in the city, and I knew I didn't have a choice. I'd already blown through a $118 on gas and food.

Knowing I probably smelled worse than a steer in the heat of a summer day, I stopped at the place advertised on the billboard, which was in Hoboken, New Jersey. I booked a "residence room" which meant there was a kitchen. Well, not a kitchen exactly. In the corner of the room was a tiny fridge, a sink, a few mismatched dishes in the cupboards, and a little counter, which had a small hot-plate. The fake wood walls were probably the nicest feature, but the leaky faucet was going to drive me nuts. I'd have to check with the front desk about getting that fixed. The room was disgusting compared to my room back home, but I needed a place to sleep.

After I took a shower, I smiled at my reflection and practiced what I thought would be good poses for a modeling company. I laughed at myself and put on my best jeans and T-shirt, locked up my new 'home,' and climbed into my truck to go find this Ford Modeling company.

Driving in New York City was insane. The place was so fucking huge! And crowded. And busy. I found the address after nearly crashing half a dozen times from checking the map and not seeing the yellow taxis who had probably gotten their licenses out of a box of Cracker Jacks.

The giant building, where the company was located, almost sent me packing. I was actually intimidated. And what was I doing here to be a model anyway? This was stupid. But I found myself in the elevator and going up before I knew it. Yeah, I was an impulsive one. Always had been.

The girl at the front desk had me drooling. She was hot. In fact, looking around the place, all the women were hot. Okay, so maybe this wasn't so stupid after all.

"Can I help you?" she asked, snapping me out of my drooling stage. She was completely unaffected by *my* looks, which hurt a bit. Back home, my whole life, people were always checking me out.

"Uh, yeah." I pulled Penny's business card out of my back pocket and showed the girl, her large green eyes making my knees weak. "I'm here to see Penny Paulson."

"Uh-huh. You and a dozen others," she said, nodding at the bank of chairs behind me. I turned and looked. Sure enough there were about a dozen people sitting in seats. There were a number of drop dead gorgeous women, and about an equal number of guys, sitting there; everyone was dressed much better than I was. "Take a seat."

I shoved the card back into my pocket and went to take a seat next to a blonde. Right away I pegged her as a bimbo as she sat there popping the fruity gum she was chewing. Her over-glossed lips turned up in a small, conceited smile as I sat down. I started checking out the other guys. Two guys had that goofy Marlboro Man mustache look. Okay, I was slightly jealous of those guys again. One guy, it seemed, thought he was John Travolta from *Saturday Night Fever*, decked out in a white disco suit. I looked at my jeans and rubbed my chin, feeling wildly out of place. Everyone had photos in their hands, many had fancy leather cases to showcase them. One guy was holding a leather binder and he was flipping through it. I saw that they were all pictures of himself that looked like they were already ads in magazines. I was nothing like these guys.

I was just about to get up and leave when the door behind the girl opened and Penny Paulson stepped out. Everyone looked at the door; two guys stood up.

She had a couple of words with the green-eyed girl that was guarding her door before she scanned the group. A huge smile burst onto her face when her eyes came to rest on me.

"Jack Stevens! I can't believe you came!" she said, her eyes bugging out.

"Well, you said—" I said, glancing around nervously, noticing that everyone's eyes were on me.

"Yeah, yeah. Please, come on in," she said, waving me into her office.

The guy that was paging through his binder snapped his book closed and leaned back and muttered under his breath, "Fuckin' A!"

The gum popper that I was seated next to said, "I knew you had the look the second you stepped through that door. Good luck."

I stood and wiped my sweaty hands on my jeans and turned to the gum-snapper. "Thanks," I said and walked over to where Penny was waiting, passing the two other guys who were still standing, and I noticed that I was taller than them.

"You should have called first, but I'm so happy you came," Penny said, closing the door to her office.

"Oh, I'm sorry, I was just—"

"No problem, no problem," she said, sitting behind her large white desk. "Sit, sit."

She motioned toward an orange chair, so I sat, and she was a flurry of activity and words. Shuffling papers, making calls to guys named 'Pierre,' and 'Miguel.' Then I signed some *provisional* something-or-other and the green-eyed girl was called into the office.

"Denise, can you please walk Mr. Stevens down to the studio for test shots?" Penny asked.

"Of course, Ms. Paulson. File?" She extended her hand over the desk, jangling an armload of silver bracelets. Penny handed her a file with the papers she'd filled out while we talked and the papers I had just signed.

Five minutes later, I was standing in front of a white back drop and some guy named Pierre, who acted a lot like a girl, was literally gushing with an accent about my 'glorious height', 'fabulous hair', and 'stunning bone structure'. He was snapping shots at me with a fancy looking camera, in between fussing with my hair and calling over his shoulder to another guy about lights and panels and stuff. And then he had me stand one way and then another. Having me pretend a few emotions. *"You're thinking about your girlfriend and you can't wait to have her in your arms." "You see the most gorgeous woman across the room." "You're hanging with the guys, watching a sports game."*

"Darling, would you mind taking off your shirt. We need to get a few shots of your physique."

"Um, you want me to take off my clothes?" I asked, stunned.

"I've seen it all before, sweetheart," he cooed, rolling his eyes.

I looked at the other people standing around. They all looked completely bored. I pulled my shirt out of my jeans, yanked it off, and handed it to the assistant who stood with his hand impatiently held out to me.

"Oh my," Pierre sighed. "Okay, I've seen a lot. *Now* I've seen it all." I felt really self-conscious as Pierre's eyes raked over my pecs and abs. I was proud of my six-pack, but to have another guy eye me like the girls did was not why I did two hundred sit-ups every night. Pierre shook it off and lifted his camera, clicking a few dozen more pictures, having me turn this way and that.

When we were done, the assistant tossed me my shirt and started turning all the lights off. Pierre packed up his camera and went about his business. Denise was back at my side, and we were headed back to elevator.

"I think Pierre got a lot of great shots back there," she said.

"Thanks," I said. "It was the strangest thing I've ever done."

"Well, you were a natural. Then again, Penny's got an exceptional eye. She knows."

We stood awkwardly for a minute. She pressed the down button, not the up button to go back up to Penny's office. "We should have the test shots back in a couple of days. It's already Thursday, so I wouldn't expect the test shots back until Monday. Penny will look them over and we'll give you a call. Your number is—" She opened the file and looked down the sheet where Penny wrote down all my info. "Two-oh-one?

Oh, Hoboken," she grimaced, wrinkling her nose. *Jeez*, I thought. I knew it stunk there, but hell, I didn't have much money.

"Yeah, for now. Staying at a hotel there. But I didn't know it would be so far. Know where I could find a cheap place to stay in this town?"

"Town?" she giggled, making me feel even more stupid than I had since arriving here. "This is a city. And nothing is cheap. You're better off in Hoboken." The elevator dinged and opened. I stepped back so Denise could step in. "No thank you, I'll be going up."

"Right. Sure. Of course," I nodded and stepped into the elevator, then pressed the button for the lobby.

I left the building in a daze. I'd just driven for three days and nearly two thousand miles on some wild goose chase, and I was given the bum's rush. Did I get the job or not?

I spent the next couple of days playing goofy tourist which would have been more fun if I was with someone. I saw the Empire State Building, the Brooklyn Bridge, and the Statue of Liberty. It was weird having read about those places in school and not giving two fucks about any of them, and now I was walking around looking at them all.

However, through the excitement at the famous stuff I was seeing, I was kind of missing home. People were just plain rude here. I was missing the midwestern manners. You know, like when someone bumped into you, they should apologize. Here someone would bump into me, and then they'd look at me like I was diseased and had gotten in their way. As annoying as a small town could be with everyone knowing everything about you, and everything you did got back to your parents before you got home, being somewhere where no one knew who you were and didn't care was rather lonely. I thought it would be liberating, but I just felt blah. But I couldn't go back home now. *Now* I had something to prove.

CHAPTER 3

Tuesday rolled around and I pulled out Penny's business card and dialed the office.

"Ford. Penny Paulson's office. This is Denise."

"Um, hi, Denise? This is Jack. Jack Stevens."

"Jack. Hi, how are you?"

"Can I talk to Pen – er – Ms. Paulson?" I asked.

"She's in a meeting for the next couple of hours. Can I have her call you?" she offered.

"Sure. The number I gave her last week is good. Do you know when I'll start working?"

She was quiet. "Look, clearly you don't know how this business works. You need headshots, pound the pavement, put in your dues. You don't just show up and work in front of the camera."

"Yeah, but—"

"Look," she interrupted. She must be a New Yorker. Rude. "You're hot. You have a chance. Want some advice?"

"Yeah. Please," I begged, spotting a cockroach squeeze under the baseboard in the shit hole I'd been living in for the past few days. Fuck! I left a clean home for this. No job and a roach infested hell.

"Get a job. A flexible job, like waiting tables. Hit up all the agencies. Not just the big ones. You'll need to get experience in the smaller ones first. And even those are a bitch to get into. You need headshots. I'll talk to Penny about letting you use the test shots. They turned out well."

She stopped talking, but I had only just started to process what she was saying. "So, I'm not going to be working for Ford?"

"It's not my call. It's Penny's, but I've been sitting at this desk long enough—"

"But she said that the company was looking for more male models with my kind of look."

"I'll have Penny call you."

The line went silent. *Fuck!* I'm thousands of miles from home. Running down my college savings. And unemployed.

Get a job. I heard Denise's words echo in my head. A *flexible* job.

I walked down to the front desk of the hotel, slapped a quarter down on the desk and took a newspaper back to my room. I spent the next hour combing through the classifieds, the whole time willing the phone to ring with Penny on the other end telling me that I was in.

But that call never came. By the week's end, I had spent a thousand dollars of my four grand. Most of it shelled on actual living expenses, and a stupid amount on damn pay-per-view porn. And I had to learn how to do laundry. Shit.

The drip in the faucet only added to my frustration. I went to the front desk expecting to see the bald guy I had seen there all week. Instead there was a hot babe sitting, staring into a small TV wearing a name tag that said 'Stephanie'.

"Hi, Stephanie. Who do I talk to about getting the faucet fixed in my room?" She laughed at me without looking up.

"Honey, this ain't the Ritz Carlton," she said in a nasally, conceited tone.

I cleared my throat and she glanced at me through her clearly fake lashes. I flashed her my best smile and said, "Can you point me to the wrenches maybe? I can probably get it fixed in five minutes flat."

Her mood seemed to change and a coy smile spread across her face as she started to fluff her hair. "You can fix stuff?" she asked.

I shrugged. "Sure. Shouldn't be a problem. I'm pretty good with my hands."

"I bet you are," she whispered, her eyes roaming over my chest without trying to hide it. "Come on. I'll show you where the maintenance closet is," she said, slipping out from behind the desk.

She led me down a hallway, shaking her fine ass, barely covered by a pair of jean shorts like the ones that Daisy Duke wore from that new show *The Dukes of Hazzard.* An image of me and Stephanie all tangled up in the back of the Plymouth Road Runner that Daisy drove in the show ran through my mind and I was hard as a rock. Sex in cars was the hottest thing. Okay, maybe not *the* hottest, but up there. Moments later, Stephanie opened the door to a closet, purposefully pushing her gorgeous tits into me, which were barely covered by her plaid shirt unbuttoned and only tied in the front, another Daisy Duke fashion statement.

She glanced down to my jeans, and my tent didn't go unnoticed. "Is there *anything* you see that can *help* you?" She slowly blinked her bright blue eyes at me.

What can I say? She asked for it. A second later and I had her pressed up against the wall. One hand swiftly pulled the shirt open and pinched her already taut nipple. The other hand had efficiently unbuttoned her barely-there-shorts and I drove a finger into her dripping slit.

"Mmmm," she groaned in my ear. "You *are* good with your hands." She pressed her chest into my hand, and tilted her hips into my other hand.

"Are you just as good with your mouth?" I asked back.

She gasped and pushed me off of her. Before I could register what was going on, she slapped me. My cheek burned.

"Jackass!" she said pulling up her shorts and fixing her top. *Seriously? That name again?* "When you're done, replace the tools," she barked. I watched her march down the hall swinging that sweet ass at me. She shot back one last glance, and I would swear on a stack of bibles she was smirking. She was one hell of a dick tease.

I fixed the leaky faucet in my room with a wrench and some plumbers tape.

The next day, when the hotel's manager found out about the repair, he offered me a job as a maintenance man in exchange for the room. The work was flexible, and easy enough, from repairing holes in the walls and broken windows, to fixing faucets and getting air conditioners to work. And staying for free, I was saving $225 a week.

Stephanie quickly became my biggest fan. She wasn't a dick tease for long. A couple of days after our first encounter and her prancing about, wearing low cut tops and scraps of cloth for shorts, she came knocking at my door.

I opened the door wearing nothing but jeans, just out of the shower, toweling my hair. Stephanie leaned on the door jam and her jaw literally dropped. Loved that reaction when chicks got a good look at my cut biceps and washboard abs. Made the hours of sit ups and push ups worth it. Bet she was wishing she'd let me finish what we'd started back in that maintenance closet.

"Um, Sal wants you to fix something," she mumbled.

"Oh yeah?" I asked, casually flexing my biceps as I continued to rub my hair with the towel.

"Yeah, only I forgot what it was." She stepped inside and closed the door.

"Well, I'm pretty sure my room's all good."

"Things *do* look good here," she said, standing a few inches in front of me. God, I was so hard. My dick's had nothing but my hand for the past few months and I wanted to sink it into that sweet pussy I'd gotten a nice feel for a few days ago. But she had called me a Jackass, and that hurt. It was my turn.

"So where do things need fixin'?" I asked in a low voice.

"I guess it's me. I'm sorry for last week," she said leaning up against the wall. She bit her lip in a classic *come fuck me* way. Oh, how I wanted to.

I tossed the towel on the bed and placed my hands on either side of her head against the wall she was leaning on. "You don't say?" I replied, playing her little game.

"Uh-huh. I was kind of a tease. That wasn't very nice."

I glanced sideways at the bed. "No, that wasn't very nice." I ran a finger along her jaw and down her neck and continued until my finger reached between her breasts…her gorgeous, round breasts "How can you make it up to me?"

Her eyes traveled down my chest and abs. I watched her chest heave as her breathing grew heavier. When her eyes reached the top of my pants, she licked at her lips. *Fuck! She wants to give me head! And I didn't even ask.* And after she was so 'put out' when I mentioned it the other day, calling me a Jackass. Hell yeah I was gonna let her do it.

When she looked up at me, I glanced down at the top of my pants. She took the hint and went to work undoing the button and zipper, then dropped to her knees. She tugged down my jeans and her small, soft hands took hold of my huge, hard cock as it sprang from its confines.

"Commando, huh?" she asked, noting that I hadn't any underwear on.

Truth was, I'd run out of clean ones and had to figure out how to do laundry yet, but she seemed turned on by it, so I played it off. "You know," I said shrugging. "The 'big guy' needs to breathe."

She got right to work and sucked me off, working me good. But just as my balls started to tighten and I was ready to explode, she pulled my dick out of her mouth and pumped it with her fist until I came all over her neck and tits. *Holy. Fuck! That was so hot!*

"I should probably get cleaned up. I can't go back to the desk like this." She untied her shirt and dropped it to the floor, then with her back to me, slid her shorts over her ass, and continued naked into my shower. Needless to say, I joined her for my first shower fuck. God, I loved being out from under my parents roof.

Stephanie and I played all sorts of wicked little games, and just when I'd started thinking that Stephanie and I were an item, her *boyfriend* came home. He'd been gone for ten weeks to basic training for the Army. And when he came back, he brought a ring. He fucking proposed to Stephanie right in the motel lobby. Just my luck that I was getting a bucket of ice at that time to witness the whole sappy proposal. She quit the next day.

It was fine. Really. I didn't have the time for a girlfriend anyway. Especially one as high maintenance as Stephanie.

CHAPTER 4

Three months later, I was still living in the cockroach infested motel. The residents were mostly a mix of freshly divorced old guys, sleazy business types who were also cheating on their wives, and a few women—one of whom I was more than a little convinced was a hooker, and not the young, hot, hard-body kind either. She was always touching me and trying to get me to invite her in, but truthfully, she smelled like booze and Ben-Gay, and her saggy boobs didn't do it for me. My neighbor was this guy named Gerry. He was a vet from the Vietnam War and was having a tough time getting a full time job. He said he was a drifter and hoping to find the *right* gig. I thought the problem was bigger than that, but I didn't dare say a word. He was usually polishing his guns and grumbling. All I needed was to piss him off and have him unload a handgun at me. All in all, I couldn't complain. I was staying without paying.

Because my repair guy gig at the dumpy motel of messed up misfits didn't pay, just gave me a place to live for free, I followed Denise's advice and got a job at a diner, but could only get hired as a bus boy. I'd hoped it would be like Mel's Diner on the TV show *Alice*. In some ways, the job was similar, the head cook was rude and gruff like Mel, but the waitresses weren't nearly as funny. They were nice though, so that was something. The money wasn't great. In fact, it sucked.

I got by on cheap plates at the diner, and the tiny paycheck covered my costs of getting into the city—but barely. On my days off, two a week, I was able to make it into the city to visit modeling agencies and try to get 'representation' so that I could get a good paying gig and get out of the nightmare that had become my life. I never thought I'd miss my crappy job stocking shelves at Thompson's Market. I was missing home more and more as the weeks passed. But I couldn't go home a failure.

Today was one of my days off, so I was headed into the city. I parked my truck for ten bucks, which left three bucks in my pocket, and made my way to an agency that had been referred to me last week. It was a newer agency, supposedly put together by some big players from established agencies that came together to create this new company, WMW Models, Inc.

I walked up to the desk and signed in as I had grown accustomed to doing. The secretary looked up and smiled. "Headshots?" she asked.

I handed her my envelope.

The receptionist slid the photos out of the envelope. "You have just the test session?" she scowled.

I shrugged. "Yeah." Denise was great. She'd gotten permission for me to use a few of my test shots as headshots, but the reprints were not cheap. One day, I'd have to find a photographer and get a real set of shots, but at the moment, I didn't have the money.

"Have a seat and fill this out." She handed me my envelope and a clipboard with the standard fill-in-the-blank sheet of basic info. I took my seat along with the other hopefuls. I surveyed the others with their fat portfolios of work and, again, felt like a fish out of water.

A half an hour later I was about ready to ditch the place when I was called.

"Hi, Jack, I'm William," he said, escorting me into his office. He was a tall man, almost my height and dressed all in black, and had a beard that made him look like one of the BeeGees. He took his seat behind a large wooden desk. There was nowhere for me to sit, so I stood there nervously as William looked at my photos and read over my stats sheet.

"This says you're six foot four?" he asked, looking me up and down.

"Yeah," I nodded.

"Have you ever done runway?"

"No, sir."

"Let me see you walk," he said leaning back in his chair.

Nervously, I straightened up and walked from one side of the room to the other. I felt as stupid as all get out.

"Walk to the door, turn and come back," he instructed, folding his hands together and pointing his index fingers up and tapping them on his chin.

Was this guy trying to look at my ass? I thought nervously. Most of the time, I walked into the office, the guy or gal looked at my stats and photos and said 'Thanks, we'll keep you in mind,' they kept my photos and I left. I never had to walk around.

"Again. Less movement in your arms and shoulders, this time. Stare straight ahead, no emotion."

I repeated the little walk to the door and back to his desk. He narrowed his eyes and nodded.

"What other jobs do you have lined up in the next couple of weeks?"

"Just bussing tables and the repairs at the motel." He looked at me blankly. "At The Corner Diner and the motel I'm staying at in Hoboken," I explained, pointing at my stats sheet.

"I'm talking about modeling jobs."

"Oh, um—" I stammered, feeling about two inches tall. "Nothing," I got out. "At the moment," I added hastily.

"So, here's the deal. You need some coaching, but I think you'll be a good match for walking with Rebecca. I need you to clear your schedule for this week to work with the team, next Tuesday is the fitting, and the show will be Friday night. If it goes well, there's another show the following weekend. The pay isn't camera work, but it's something. You get paid after the show. No advances. It'll get your résumé started at least. And you'll have some photos to add to these test shots."

I stood shocked. I'd just gotten a booking. I was being hired for my first modeling gig. Three months of twice a week coming into the city, visiting five or six agencies every week and I was finally getting a shot. I didn't know how to react. "Right on! Thank you, sir," I said extending my hand to shake his and seal the deal.

"Don't thank me yet, kid. Runway is no picnic. See you at ten o'clock tomorrow morning. Get plenty of rest, you're gonna need it."

I laughed inside, thinking to myself, *Walking? How hard can it be?* But I schooled the sarcasm and said, "Yes, of course. Ten o'clock. I'll be here."

William pulled out papers, rattling off some contract jargon, which all seemed fine to me. I signed a three month contact, to be reviewed at the end of the term. I left the office committing the date to memory: Tuesday, September 18, 1979. My first modeling gig was booked. I was on my way.

I got cocky with the booking and went to the diner and turned in my notice. It wasn't two weeks, but the manager of the diner said he understood. He'd known that I'd come to New York to do just this. The waitresses were gushing and telling me they'd look for me in magazines and billboards.

At the motel, I told the manager I wouldn't be able to do any repairs for the next couple of weeks on account of the gig. He said he'd have to start charging me rent again. My savings was nearly gone, but I was about to get a paycheck, so I didn't care.

CHAPTER 5

I showed up on time that Wednesday morning to work with the 'team' William mentioned. They had me walking, posing, stopping, turning, doing all sorts of queer stuff to show off clothing. I felt like a complete dork. Three days of working with this team, and every night I went home exhausted.

The following Tuesday I showed up for the fitting and felt like the biggest moron that walked the planet. They tested all sorts of colors and outfits ultimately deciding on three different looks, each outlandish and something that you would never be caught dead in on the streets or in a club. The tailor made markings and adjustments while I stood there like a god-damned mannequin.

Out of nowhere, a tall, beautiful blonde walked up to us with absolute conviction of her importance. I recognized her instantly from magazine covers and billboards. Strangely, I no longer felt six-four. She was almost as tall as I was, bossy, and freakishly intimidating to everyone around her. "They've paired us up. Lemme see your walk," she ordered, crossing her arms in front of her.

The man marking the bottom of the pants moved back so I could walk for this Amazon woman before me. With the team I'd been working with for the past few days in my head, I took several paces, turned, posed, and walked back to the blonde.

She looked me up and down through narrowed eyes. "Now with me."

I put my arm out for her and she took it. We marched, I stood back to let her pose, I did my thing, she took my arm and we marched back.

"Hmm," she huffed. "I think they got it right this time. See you Friday."

And as quickly as she arrived, she turned and left. The tailor went back to working on my pants as if a six-foot tornado hadn't just spun around this space. "What the hell was that?" I said.

The tailor shook his head, "Rebecca Campbell. One of a kind."

On Friday, I showed up an hour early to the address William gave me for the runway show. After meeting Rebecca Campbell for less than two minutes the other day, I was in no way gonna piss her off. But wouldn't you know it, she was a full two hours *late* to the event causing quite a buzz among the coordinators and other models. When she finally showed, she was clearly drunk and her eyes were red. I started to freak out. She was tanked and if she fell, surely everyone would blame me. I'd be back on the highway to Colorado before you could say 'runway.' Her manager was fuming, and whisked her off muttering about needing a miracle worker.

We ran the dress rehearsal runs, but Rebecca wasn't on the stage with me. I had to make like she was there which was so beyond awkward. I was starting to panic, but William told me I'd done well, that Rebecca was a "consummate professional," and we'd be fine. I had nothing to go by, so I just prayed for the best at show time.

Not sure what they did to clean her up. A lot of Visine for her eyes, I guessed. And I could smell the coffee and mint mixed with booze on her breath. Ultimately, the show went off without a hitch. Rebecca played the crowds like a pro, even giving me the center stage for my own applause. I had mixed feelings about the whole thing. There was a certain excitement about walking in front of people applauding and hundreds of flashbulbs going off in my face, but it was also rather terrifying, because all of those flashes made you rather blind. I thought back to the photo session with Pierre taking the test shots, and as awkward as that was, it was more comfortable than the live show.

After the hoopla, back in my own clothes, I was talking to a few of the other models about heading out to get something to eat. I was starving and totally up for it when Rebecca's manager came up to me.

"Jack Stevens. Nice to meet you formally. William was right with this one. Gotta hand it to the man," she said, grinning. "Frannie DiMarco," she said, introducing herself, sticking her hand out to me, which I took and shook. "I'm Miss Campbell's manager. Do you have a sec?"

I looked around to see the other models stare. Some were clearly pissed, a couple were in awe. "Uh, sure," I muttered. "I'll catch you guys another time," I said to the group and followed Frannie to a quiet corner.

"So, William says you're living in Hoboken?" she asked. Man these model industry people sure were interested in my living conditions.

"Yeah."

"Do you like it?"

I scoffed, "No. It's sh—I mean, I've stayed in nicer places."

"What is your lease like?"

"I'm week to week."

"Did you secure next week yet?"

I shook my head 'no'. "I usually sign for the next week on Saturdays."

She nodded. "I have an idea. Would you mind a roommate?"

"No, I guess not," I shrugged, confused. Surely she wasn't suggesting...

She turned on her heel and I got the notion I was supposed to follow her, so I did.

I quickly caught up to her and she led us into a lounge where Rebecca sat on a bright yellow leather sofa. She had small headphones on her head and a small device that looked like it was playing a cassette tape, with the word WALKMAN scrawled on the front of it, sitting on her lap. The music was blaring so loudly through the ridiculously small headphones that I could hear it from the doorway. I recognized the song as being one of ABBA's. Jenny and her friend, Suzie, used to listen to those records all the time.

Frannie walked up to Rebecca and pulled the headphones off her head. "Would you consider him?"

Consider me for what? She *was the roommate?*

"Of course you'd bring a guy," Rebecca shot back to Frannie.

Rebecca cocked an eyebrow and looked me up and down. I looked her over as well. She was beautiful. Her skin was bright and smooth. Her eyes were an interesting light brown, and almost clear, except for a trace of the redness and puffiness from crying. They reminded me of a necklace that Jenny used to wear. She said it was amber or something like that. Rebecca's blonde hair was sleek and pulled back into a long pony-tail now.

She stood and I swallowed hard. This was so bizarre. I felt like I was in an episode of the Twilight Zone and that Rod Sterling was going to pop out of the hallway.

"Tell me about yourself," she said calmly.

I had no idea what was happening. I looked from Frannie to Rebecca and back to Frannie. "Look, I don't know what's going on here—"

"Apparently I need a babysitter, or excuse me, a roommate," Rebecca interrupted herself rolling her eyes at Frannie. "Do you have a girlfriend? Or a boyfriend?" she asked.

I almost fell over. A *boyfriend?* Was she serious? Rebecca sat tapping her foot at me waiting for an answer. "Right now I'm single. But girls, all the way, man."

"Forget it." Rebecca said and took her seat back on the yellow leather sofa and slipped her headphones back on.

Frannie turned to me and said, "Can you give us a minute? There's a kitchen across the hall. Help yourself to whatever you want."

"Uh, sure." I backed out of the room and went in search of the kitchen. I was starving, so it was a good thing. And I wasn't going to have to pay for it, which was even better. But the kitchen was a major disappointment. The fridge only had fruits and veggies and some *Sweet & Low Yogurt.* Even the drinks were girly. Pink cans of TaB cola, uh – no thank you. *Boyfriend.* Is that what I'm going to have to put up with if I do this modeling thing? Pussy food and people thinking I was some homo?

I swallowed my pride and grabbed a couple of carrot sticks and sat in a chair wondering if any of this made sense. I was supposed to be a fourth generation rancher and here I was sitting as a model after a runway show in New York City. I had been getting my picture taken by a guy who clearly digs other guys. I'm eating fucking carrot sticks, and considering drinking a can of TaB.

Just then Rebecca walked into the kitchen and stood in front of me. "Fine you can move in."

"What if I don't want to move in?" I shot back. I glanced behind her and saw Frannie looking at me. She placed her hands in front of her like she was praying I would say yes. *What in the hell was going on here?*

"Look. It's free. It's clean. I'm clean. You better be."

Frannie nodded her head at me.

"Where do you live?" I asked.

"Park Avenue. You in, or what?"

"Are you serious? I have to get my truck and my stuff."

"My building doesn't have parking. You'll have to get rid of your truck.

"I'm *not* getting rid of my truck."

"Aw, fuck! Are you for real?" she groaned.

I didn't know how to answer that. For starters, nothing felt real right now. I'd just done my first real modeling gig, a fucking runway show, and now I was talking to a super-model. One loaded with attitude. Attitude I used to have in Colorado. I stood, my face set. I was not backing down. I'd had enough of this shit.

"Fine, if you want to throw away fifty bucks or more a day parking your precious *truck*, that's your business. But my building doesn't have parking." She turned to a drawer in the kitchen and pulled out a small note pad and pencil. She started writing furiously on it. "Here's my address and phone number—in case you get lost. See you tomorrow," she said, thrusting the piece of paper at me.

Frannie stood at the door, silently clapping her hands and looking as happy as Jim Lange making a connection on *The Dating Game.*

Really? Two steps forward, one step back. I finally get a modeling gig, and an opportunity at a nicer place to live than the roach motel, but a girl roommate? One who didn't want me around? Me? Jack Stevens? Even this small town boy has standards.

"I have to think about it," I said in my most grown up voice, taking the piece of paper.

Great. I'm being backed into a corner and given some punk kid to be my babysitter. *Jack Stevens.* Even his name wreaks country bumpkin. Bet he hasn't even graduated high school. Some dropout wanna-be. I'm twenty-fucking-five years old! Not that I look a day over nineteen. I'm a successful supermodel. My face has been on Cosmopolitan and Vogue magazine covers and billboards in Times Square.

And now, because Dan walked out on me this morning, and with my *history*, the powers that be are putting me between a rock and hard place. Forcing me to have a roommate. Or I'll have to find another agency. Bet they'll turn this pretty boy into their own personal narc. I don't need one. Just because the love of my life has left doesn't mean I'm going to fall apart and run to the dealer on the next corner. I may run to the liquor store, but that's it.

CHAPTER 6

I woke up around ten o'clock on Saturday morning. Sleeping in felt great. I stretched and grabbed a smoke. As I lit up, I spotted the scrap of paper with Rebecca's address that she had given me last night. Park Avenue. Suddenly, I burst out laughing. The theme song for *Green Acres* ran through my head and Eva Gabor, or was it Zsa Zsa? I always got those two confused. *Da-dah Da-dah-dah something about Park Avenue,* I hummed in my head. Man, I sucked at lyrics. Good thing I didn't come to New York to be a singer.

Right. I'm gonna move in with that arrogant bitch. Not happenin'. She was so full of herself and she clearly didn't want me moving in. Why did Frannie think this was a good thing? But looking around the shit hole that I'd been living in for the past three months, maybe it wasn't a bad thing. I'd been ignoring the peeling paint, the thin walls, and the stale stench of the carpeting. I mean, it was pretty much all I could afford, and I didn't have another choice. But now, another choice was literally handed to me last night.

I finished my smoke, ran all of my laundry, and four hours later checked out of the motel. Fighting the famous New York City traffic and cabs, I found myself parked in a parking lot collecting a ticket from some guy who smelled like the urinals at Folsom Field. I silently prayed that my truck would be okay. My 1973 Ford F-100 was my baby. My brother Jim helped me rebuild the engine, I'd lost my virginity in it, and gotten laid more times than I could count in it. She'd gotten me all the way to New York.

I stuffed the ticket in my back pocket, and pulled out the address Rebecca had given me. I looked at my map, made a couple mental notes then slung my duffle bag over my shoulder and headed in the direction I thought I was supposed to go. It wasn't until a few blocks later that I realized the numbers were going up, not down, so I turned around and back tracked. Half a mile later, and nearly getting run over by a taxi or two, I finally found her building; a large, dark red awning looming over a heavy-set doorman standing guard.

He looked me up and down, and warily eyed my duffle bag as I walked up. I had half a mind to head back to my truck and go back to Colorado. The snobby attitude of the doorman and the dirty smells of the streets and car exhaust were making me homesick for the sweet smelling air of the Colorado Rockies. But I had a contract now. I had to stay.

I reached for the handle of the door, but was effectively blocked by the uniformed man. "Can I help you?" he asked, bringing me back to New York.

"Um, yeah, I'm here to see Rebecca. I'm moving in." I started to walk past him to the open the door.

"Sure you are. Look kid, you should move along."

"No, I swear." I pulled out the scrap of paper that she'd scrawled her address on. "She gave me her address. This is her building, right?"

He smirked at me. "Don't make me call the cops, kid."

"Can you call her or something?"

With a face of stone, he calmly replied, "I don't even know if she lives here."

My jaw dropped. He had to be messing with me. She was beautiful. You didn't miss a girl like that. "Seriously? She's about my height. Long blonde hair? Gorgeous eyes? She's a famous model."

I looked at the paper again and saw her phone number. "Do you have a phone? I'll call her. You'll see."

Without even looking at me, he said, "Pay phone is on the corner." He jerked his head to the opposite corner where there was a phone booth.

I trudged off, adjusting my bag on my shoulder and digging out a dime to call the number on the scrap of paper. Three minutes later, the doorman was holding the door open for me looking more than a little annoyed.

I got off of the elevator onto the 22nd floor and saw a door wide open, just as Rebecca said she would do. Light and music was flooding into the hallway. Hesitantly, I walked to the door and stepped inside, then closed the door behind me. I leaned back and looked around—stunned.

The song *Hot Stuff* by Donna Summer surrounded me, making me laugh remembering that this very song was playing on the car radio after I had talked to Penny and quit Thompson's Market. I looked over at the giant speakers that were blaring the tune; a high end stereo system. And right next to that, a huge record collection. *Nice!* Looking around the apartment, it was like something you'd see on a prime time TV drama that Jenny used to watch. Yup, Rebecca was loaded. She was an inspiration. I hoped I'd be able to afford something like this next year on my own.

Everywhere I looked, white, modern furnishings were meticulously placed and everything was as neat as a pin. Low, white, leather sofas with straight lines that looked rather uncomfortable. And the arms of the chairs were wooden, more like end tables attached to the piece of furniture. Funky shaped, white plastic chairs with circles punched in them arranged around a glass dining table. The floor was a thick white carpeting. Silver domes were attached to the wall with light coming out from behind them. This was a far cry from the roach motel, or my parents house with paneling, peeling paint, and wallpaper, furnishings that were broken or worn to within an inch of their useful lives. I decided to slip my boots off and leave them by the door.

Suddenly, Rebecca was walking into the room, and seeing her was almost more shocking than the apartment. She was wearing low slung, loose pants and a lacy, black bra. Nothing else. Her hair was wrapped up in a towel propped up on her head. Presumably, she'd just come out of the shower and had no makeup on, yet was perhaps even more beautiful than when I had seen her both times before. She was sipping on a martini glass as she entered, and dancing to the music.

I was suddenly desperate for a cigarette. I reached into my pocket, pulled out the box, and started to shake one out.

"Nuh-uh. Not in my place you don't. I'm not a smoker, and if you want to live here, you won't be one either. Those things will kill you, ya know. Find another vice—a clean one," she scolded, boring her eyes into the pack of Marlboros in my hand.

What? She was one of *those* people? Yeah, smoking was on the decline, but seriously, what was the big deal? All those movements to stop smoking because some Surgeon General said it's bad for you and a group of people had this idea that breathing in the air from my cigarette would make them sick. My whole family smoked and we're all fine. But the look on Rebecca's face said she was not going to back down.

"Um, sorry," I muttered, shoving the pack back into my pocket. *Fuck!* Now I had to find a way to quit. This whole New York thing was just getting better and better.

"And, I'm not sure what ideas you may have socked away in your head, but there will be no sex. So, if your overactive eighteen year old brain has any designs in that arena, you can turn your cute ass around and get out."

"Yes. I mean no. I mean, I wasn't thinking that at all. I mean you're beautiful and what guy wouldn't want to—but, no. I like brunettes anyway."

A bizarre smirk hit her lips, which she quickly tucked away, resuming her stonewall face.

"Your room is the first door on the right. The bathroom is across the hall from there. Keep your bathroom clean, and the toilet seat down."

Yes, sir!

"Can I get you a drink?" she offered, pointing behind me to a long table loaded with every kind of liquor you could imagine.

Okay, I have whiplash now. Scolding me and barking orders one minute and offering me a drink the next? Is this what it's going to be like living with her?

"Um, I guess, yeah? What have you got?"

"Whatever you'd like," she said, knocking back the rest of her martini. She sauntered over and started to make herself another one. The song on the record changed and now Donna Summer was belting *Bad*

Girls, and Rebecca was in full rockin' mode acting like Ms. Summer herself, oblivious to me.

I grabbed a can of Budweiser from the tiny fridge under the table that held all the booze and headed off to check out my new room. I was about to say something to Rebecca, but she was in her own little world.

As far as bedrooms went, this one was good. I mean real good. It was much like the rest of the place, modern and clean lines. But where the living room was whites and light color woods, this room was dark woods and creams. The bed was on a solid dark-wood box, and looked to be very sturdy. I dropped my bag on the floor next to the matching dresser and set the can of beer on the bedside table. I laid down on the very comfortable bed for a minute and considered my incredibly weird last few months.

I had been a stock boy in the grocery store of a town where I didn't get the most respect, due to my family's status of less than smart kids, and a couple of bitches. Some chick sees me and gives me this crazy notion to come out to New York City and try modeling. I'm knocked down for a few months while bussing tables and fixing shit in a crappy motel. I finally got a break which lead to an offer to stay with a model who seemed perhaps more than a little off-balance. Now, here I was in a very chic place, and being pushed around by said off-balance woman. Seemed like a fucking wild dream. I wasn't sure if I wanted to wake up or not.

CHAPTER 7

Not sure how much time passed, but I had apparently fallen asleep, because the next thing I knew, Rebecca was at the door calling my name. I sat up and rubbed my face.

"Yeah? What? I'm up," I said, trying to adjust my sight to the now dark room and light spilling in from the hallway.

"Next time, use a coaster. Please," she said, marching over to the bedside table, picking up the beer can, and wiping the ring of water off.

"Yeah, sure. 'Course. Sorry," I stammered. Why was I letting this girl intimidate me? Oh yeah, she was nearly as tall as I was, a successful model with a bank account to match, and knew how to throw her weight around. And it was her place.

"I'm ordering take out. Do you like Chinese? Or pizza?" she asked, a hand perched on her hip.

"Um, whatever you want," I answered, dragging myself out of bed.

"Fine. Chinese it is," she said, and walked out.

What was this chick's problem? She offered me a place to stay, and was being a total bitch. I dragged myself out of the room and pulled my pack of Marlboros from my pocket before I remembered that I wasn't allowed to smoke in her place. Maybe I'd run downstairs and grab a quick one. I was beyond edgy. Or maybe I should just fucking quit cold turkey now. I was a man. A strong man. I could do it. I made my way back to the living room, where Marvin Gaye was now singing on the stereo system and I found Rebecca hanging up the phone.

"It should be here in about twenty minutes," she said.

I nodded and then grabbed myself a fresh beer and took a seat on a wooden chair that was all bent up and looked to be incredibly uncomfortable. I was pleasantly surprised to find it quite the opposite. "So, how long have you been modeling?" I asked, trying to make small talk.

"Since I was about eight. My first gig was for a Barbie ad in the magazines. You?"

"Oh," I laughed. "I'm not really a model. I mean, I am—now," I corrected myself, realizing how it might sound. "Some chick spotted me back home in Colorado and suggested that I come out here. I had nothing else going on, maybe community college, so I said why the hell not. Things didn't work out with that agency, but I didn't give up, and well, here I am."

"Who spotted you?" she asked casually.

"Penny Paulson. But it was a bust."

"Ah, Penny. From Ford?" she asked. I nodded. "She knows her shit. And if she saw something in you, then you made the right choice coming out here. So, if you're not with Ford, who *are* you with?" she asked, sipping something blue out of a glass now.

"William from WMW Modeling? I think they're new," I shrugged.

"WMW…" she muttered. Then her eyes grew wide. "Oh right, William Westerly! I heard he broke free from those—" she glanced at me quickly. "Well, good on William. But you mean to tell me you've never modeled before?"

I shook my head. "In fact, I'm hopin' to keep this whole thing quiet. I just want to make some money for college."

Rebecca threw her head back, laughing hysterically.

"What?" I shot at her.

"You know that William is kind of a legend in the industry, right? He's from one of the biggest, and most successful modeling agencies in the world. He's got connections up his sleeve as far as that sleeve goes, which is like your height and mine combined. You're not going to go unnoticed. Your look *is* very fresh, and if William sees your potential, you're going straight to the top."

I absorbed what Rebecca had said and downed half of my beer. I should just turn this crazy train around now and head home before I became the laughing stock of Charter Oaks.

"You seriously had no idea?" Rebecca asked, studying my face.

"No," I said, shaking my head, running my hand through my hair, feeling dumb. *Should* I have known?

"Where in Colorado are you from? Denver? Boulder?"

"I'm from Charter Oaks, Colorado. I'm from a family of ranchers outside of Boulder."

"Wow, a country bumpkin. Far out, Penny!" Rebecca slid off the sofa and headed over to the bar. I watched her assemble and shake up another blue martini. How much was this girl going to drink?

"So, you've been modeling since you were eight. How long have you been modeling?" I asked trying to figure out as much about Rebecca as I could.

"Now that's a clever way of asking a woman her age."

I shrugged.

"I'm twenty-five. Basically a 'has-been' in this business."

"What?" I choked. "No way you're twenty-five. And what do you mean, a *has been?*"

"This is a short-lived industry, kid," she stated, settling back into her spot on the sofa.

"So, am I your first roommate?" I asked.

Her features darkened. "No," she replied flatly.

We sat in silence. I totally needed that cigarette now. I had no idea how to dig myself out of the hole I'd inadvertently dug. Rebecca just stared out of the window at the lights of New York City, draining half of her freshly poured drink. I racked my brain for something to talk about, to change the subject, but came up empty.

"Danny moved out three days ago," she said quietly.

"Oh. Sorry," I managed. He must have broken her heart big time. Maybe all this drinking was a bender from his leaving her.

"We were together for six years. Then one fight... a stupid fight. My fault really. And it's over. Fuck!" she spit out through clenched teeth, then she opened up and drained her glass. She gritted her teeth some more, her jaw muscles throbbing. A tear sprung from her watery eyes and ran down her beautiful cheek.

Suddenly, the phone on the wall by the door rang, interrupting the awkward silence. Rebecca sprang off the seat, practically running to the device while wiping the tears away, and picked up the phone. "He'll be right down," she said after a second of listening, hung it up and walked over to her purse. She rummaged around and handed me a ten dollar bill. "Run downstairs and pay the delivery guy. I'll get the dishes."

I stood and set my beer down on the glass dining table, avoiding wood surfaces, and made my way down to pay the delivery guy in the lobby. Five minutes later, I was eating the best Chinese take out food I'd ever had, which was a nice change of pace from the diner food. The whole time we ate, Rebecca told me wild stories of jobs she'd done and the exotic places she'd traveled for work. I told her about growing up on a ranch in rural Colorado.

"Well," I said, standing and picking up my plate to bring to the kitchen. "The last week with getting ready for that show last night really kicked my ass. But Rebecca," I stopped. She looked up at me and blinked, a new softness on her features. "Thanks for the place to stay. It sure beats the motel."

"No problem, kid," she said, her stellar smile crossing her face. "And Rebecca is my professional name. My friends call me Becca."

Okay, it might not be so bad having him around. He's nice. Polite. Funny even. He hasn't said one word about my decorating or my drinking. And he didn't push me about the break up.

I cleared the table, marveling at how there weren't any left overs. When Dan was here, even between the two of us, there were always left overs. Jack's got quite an appetite. He's going to have to start quite a workout routine if he's going to keep that up. But then again—he's only eighteen.

I thought about back when I was 18. I was already on the cover of a dozen magazines. I was already earning five figures for a day long photo shoot. I'd met Danny when I was 18 and we started seeing each other "officially" just a year later. And then we moved in to my place a few months after that. And then the accusations, and name calling, and... Margot!!!! *Lock it up, Becca! Memory lane will get you nowhere!*

I marched over to the bar and mixed another drink.

CHAPTER 8

Acouple of weeks after I had moved in, I came home from a photo shoot that I had landed from the runway show. It was for suntan oil. I had to rub suntan oil on six hot babes. Who were wearing string bikinis. While I was tucked into a banana hammock. For three hours. And I got paid for it. This was the awesomest fucking job ever! The only glitch was one of the chicks was a real tease, finding ways to "casually" touch my junk. The photographer was all, "Dude, think about baseball, or your grandma, or the New York City subways. You cannot sport a boner in these pics." Clearly he was gay, because how does a red-blooded, heterosexual guy hang around, and *touch*, oiled up chicks, with out poppin' some wood?

I showed up at Becca's apartment so fucking hard with a plan to head straight for the shower and toss one off. Hell, I'd been choking the chicken so much lately, I was going to have hairy palms, even if I couldn't grow a decent beard or mustache. However, when I walked in to the apartment, Becca was doing some body bending shit in front of the big Zenith TV from a tape playing through her VHS player. Her ass—her tight, round ass—was high in the air. The woman on the video was saying something about *'downward dog.'* Yeah, that sounded right. I'd mount that bitch. *Shut it, Stevens,* I scolded myself. *She said no sex.* She was very clear the day I moved in that sex was out of the question. Sure, I'd been imagining what sex would be like with her since then, but probably just because she said it was a no-go.

"Um, hey," I said, kicking the door shut with my foot and shoving my hands deep in the pockets of my Levi's, balling up my fists to hide the beast ready to burst in my pants.

"Hey," she called back, looking at me through her legs. "How'd the shoot go? Isn't Andrew a hoot?"

"Uh, yeah, sure. I'm gonna take a shower. Have fun with your, whatever you're doing," I muttered and headed straight for the shower.

I started the shower, letting it heat up, although a cold shower should have been my choice, but the cold water wouldn't get the suntan oil off of me. I stripped, and my hand, still a little oily, got to work on my throbbing dick.

Suddenly the bathroom door flung open.

"Oh, shit!" Becca exclaimed. "Sorry, I thought you were—uh. Well, I washed all the towels and I just remembered you didn't have any in here. So…" Her eyes travelled down my body and rested on my once busy hand, now frozen mid-pull.

I shrugged sheepishly. I mean, I was busted. What was I gonna do?

She swallowed hard and her eyes flew up to mine. "Rough day at the office?" *Was she flirting with me?*

"Not as rough as I'd like," I said, tossing the ball back into her court as my hand started sliding back and forth again.

"Oh, you like it rough, do you?" she said with a smirk. "And here I thought you were a wholesome, midwestern, God-fearing, country boy."

"Who me? God-fearing?" I smirked back staring her right in the eyes. I must be dreaming. This was not happening.

"So, you don't get on your knees?" she asked raising an eyebrow and dropping to her knees in front of me.

"Becca…" I started, my heart pounding in my ears. I wanted this. Oh man, I wanted this. She batted my hand away and looked at my cock like it was a steak, and she'd not been eating for a week before a photo shoot. "You said…" I tried. I couldn't believe I was going to try and talk her out of giving me a blow job, but she said… and I didn't want her pissed at me, kicking me out of her place. *Oh fuck!* Her breath hitting my cock was like pouring gasoline on a bonfire.

"To hell with what I said. Clearly you have a need, and I am fully aware that a palm session isn't going to do the trick," she growled, and took my whole dick in her mouth, her hands gripping my thighs. I dropped my head back as she worked it. Slowly. Taking it all in, then pulling back to just the head and swirling her skilled tongue around the crown. She would flick her tongue on the underside—just so, then plunge forward until I was again at the back of her throat. No hands required. *Holy muther fucker!*

It wasn't but a minute later, and I was shooting off like a rocket. Spurt after powerful spurt into her mouth. And she took it all. I looked down and marveled at the blonde haired, blue-eyed super model kneeling at my johnson. She didn't seem disappointed that I didn't last. I felt like I should explain… that I had more stamina than that, but it had been a rough day… and it had been a while since I'd been with a chick…but I couldn't have formed a sentence at that moment if my life depended on it. She finished licking and cleaning me up, then stood and said "You owe me one," and left.

What the fuck does that mean? What the fuck just happened?

That night I took her out to dinner. It was the least I could do, and honestly, I didn't want to be alone with her in our apartment. While she picked at her salad, and sucked down the wine, I had a hard time eating my burger.

"So, what gives?" I asked, unable to keep the question inside.

"What gives what?" she asked back, seemingly confused.

"Uh, earlier. In my bathroom?"

"Oh, that. Look," she said, setting down her fork and taking a long sip of her wine. "I don't want a relationship. I was just horny. Yoga does that to me. I don't know why. Besides, I haven't had sex in over a week. Then I saw you walk in while I was in Downward Dog and … then I remembered your towels… and then there you were in the bathroom. I should have knocked, but—it was unfair. I'm sorry."

"It's okay," I choked out. "No problem."

"I find sex a huge release. Danny used to call me a nympho. I dunno," she shrugged. "Maybe I am. If you move out, I'll understand. But I promise, I won't do it again. Unless you want me to. Just as a friend, of course. Helping you release some stress?" A sly little smile crept onto her lips.

I sat there stunned. Was she proposing what I thought she was proposing? "Are you saying sex without being in a relationship? Just friends? Like 'fuck friends' or something?" I asked.

She thought for a second, and bobbed her head. "Yeah, I guess that's what I'm saying."

We sat and hashed out the "rules" for this *fuck friend* arrangement. No dates. No jealousy. If one of us becomes involved with another person, the fucking stops—unless the new boyfriend or girlfriend doesn't care.

She practically attacked me when we got home. She pushed me into my bedroom and tore my clothes off, then mounted me. *She* rode *me* like *her* life depended on it. Her body on display, and it was just sex. Six minutes later, we both came. She simply slid off me, tossed me a few tissues from the box on my bedside table and shot me a, "Thanks, I needed that." Seconds later, I heard her shower turn on. No cuddling. No awkward good-bye or see ya.

And the next morning, like a switch had been flipped, we were friends sipping coffee and talking about our schedule for the day. Fucking one night, and back to just friends in the morning. But it totally worked. And we'd fuck a few times a week. Neither of us getting silly about it. Most of the time it was good and rough. And fast. None of this long, take your time shit. I couldn't believe my past few weeks. I'd done my first professional runway show that lead to more work. I'd landed a sweet apartment. And now I had a fuck friend. I was the fucking man!

CHAPTER 9

May 1982

Over the next three years, Becca and I cultivated this odd relationship. On the one hand, we were fuck friends. On the other, we were each other's closest friend, almost like family. Becca's parents were big time philanthropists. Ever since Becca's career had been firmly established, and Frannie DiMarco took over managing her career, they were forever jumping onto the next public campaign. From bringing clean water and aid to remote areas of Africa, to the most recent headlines of this disease called HIV/AIDS. They had little time for Becca.

My parents had stopped taking my calls and the checks I sent home after they saw an ad I had done. It was the ad for suntan oil. My oldest sister, Sharon, found it in her Glamour magazine, and showed my dad. My dad, David Sr., was *not* impressed. Old fuck. He said that I had 'sold my soul to the devil' by putting my half naked body on display like that. My brothers and sisters gave me their congrats, but they seemed hesitant to go against Pop. My mother stayed quiet on the whole issue. I continued to send checks back home to help out my parents, but from that point on, they always sent the checks back. After two years, I stopped. It hurt too much.

Once, my sister Laura, her husband Vin, and my brother, Mike came out and visited me secretly. It was the best day of my modeling career. Not for the job, but because my brother and sister were there. I brought them to the set and they got to watch what I did. We took some fun pictures on set, too. I took them out and treated them to dinner. They said that Mom wanted to come, but she wouldn't think of crossing Dad.

I could have moved out of Becca's place after about four months of working, but it would have been a shit hole, since I didn't earn even one-tenth of what Becca did. So, I stayed. Besides, we got along really well and hung out when we were both in town. Becca continued to work, despite her previous concerns that her career was ending. She traveled a lot, and if she wasn't traveling, I was. So it was a perfect arrangement. I kept depositing money into the bank, looking forward to when I could start college. And Becca taught me all the ins and outs of this crazy business, along with correcting my grammar along the way. Apparently, I had ways of saying things that drove her nuts. Like when I say, "I want a beer bad." She'd always correct me and say, "Badly. You want it *badly*." Sometimes I would say it wrong just to annoy her. She'd gotten an English degree from Columbia and she loved to throw that in my face.

There were many perks of working as a model, the paycheck only a piece of it. It wasn't just the prestige and the parties. Or seeing your face on the cover of a magazine or on a billboard in Times Square. We got a lot of pre-release stuff. Like the Walkman that never left Becca's side; she'd gotten hers a whole two months before the thing was even to be released on the market. Why? Because she was the model selected to promo it, until they went with a younger girl anyway. The parties we went to were amazing, even if incredibly intimidating. The celebrities we met and the high-end everythings were incredible, but the never-ending supply of illicit drugs was astounding.

Becca knew several models who'd lost everything from drug use, and she was careful to keep me from it. In fact, she admitted that several years back, she had started down that road and ended up nearly losing everything herself. She said that when Danny left and she got drunk the weekend of our first runway show together, that her manager Frannie asked me to become Becca's roommate because Frannie was afraid that Becca might start using again. At any rate, I was always there to rescue her when she was in a situation, and she was there to rescue me.

I kept away from drugs, but I had certainly found my addiction. One of the biggest perks of being a 'big time model' was the never ending line of girls, many with lemon juice bleached hair and Bain de Soleil tans willing to give me a blow job or jump in the sack at a moments notice. I finally got my dream of more than one chick at a time. On more than one occasion I could be found in bed with two or three babes. Shit that was hot! Sometimes I didn't have to be there. The girls would be totally into each other, and I could sit up close, watch them kiss or eat each other out and I could play with their tits, or be fucking one. And they didn't think it made me a Jackass. Basically, I fell into this pattern of hollow meaningless one night stands.

On the one hand, it was great—no commitment. I was living every dude's dream. But on the other hand, I was getting tired of not having a steady. Half the girls I slept with were only with me because they saw my face in some ad, or heard I was a model, but had no idea who I was. The other half thought I could somehow get them *their* big break into the field. I grew more and more demanding in bed, thinking it would give me a bad rep. Instead, the girls fell even harder. And I found the high of being domineering *very* addictive.

I thought it odd that Becca never dated anyone. Clearly she was capable, having been with Danny for six years. Guess he had really done a number on her.

But mostly, Becca and I remained unattached to "that someone special." We'd still fuck like stupid kids, and the next morning we'd be back to just roommates. *So. Fucking. Awesome.* And Becca was amazing in bed. Danny was a fucking fool.

All in all, the modeling was awesome. I loved the camera work, and continued with runway jobs when they came up. Even though my big break was due to a runway show, I could have done without them. I watched these girls take tumbles, sometimes from their shoes being too tall, or the runway being too slippery. Sometimes they fell because they hadn't eaten anything in the past couple of days, or used so many laxatives that they were practically passing out. I was always a nervous wreck.

Today, Becca and I were paired up for another show, and, with her on my arm, I was guaranteed applause. Together we were a force to be reckoned with. After the shows, I always laughed at the girls as they stripped out of their costumes and wolfed down a sandwich and a milkshake. I was walking around looking for Becca so we could go grab dinner with the rest of the gang.

I rounded the corner and spied Becca arguing with Danika, the executive producer of the event. She was the one everybody feared. She controlled all the models' steps down the runway, every note blaring on the hi-fi system, every piece of boob tape, and each lock of hair. As for us guys, she mostly ignored us, for which I was grateful.

It looked to be a heated discussion, so I didn't walk in on them. Rather, I hung back around the corner and, despite my discomfort with the morality of eavesdropping on my best friend, I couldn't help myself.

"Why are you being so mean to me? I would never treat you this way," Becca pleaded.

"Becca, look. We were. It was nice, but we just didn't mesh well. If we stayed together it would have been disastrous."

Huh?

"I've never gotten over you," I heard. I wasn't sure who said it. It didn't sound like Danika. She had a raspy smoker's voice and a thick Brooklyn accent. But it didn't sound like Becca, either. The voice sounded weak and small. "I love you, Dani."

Whoa! Back the fuck up! It wasn't Danny who broke Becca's heart. It was *Dani*. Becca was a lesbian!? How had I lived with her for three years and not known? We'd fucked more than—what the fuck?! My mind was flashing through all the times I'd seen Becca with our group of friends. How she was charming and flirty with the women. Then there were her questions on the first day we'd met... but the blow jobs, and the quick fucks... I guess that's why it was always just a *fuck* and nothing more. And she never seriously dated over the past years. Neither did I, but— Becca was always saying that it would hurt too much to get her heart broken again.

It seemed as clear as day, but still as clear as mud.

"Becca, it's been three years. I still care for you, but not in that way. I'm with Margot now. We match in a way that you and I never did. Move on. Find your Margot."

Suddenly, Danika, *Dani*, was brushing past me in her authoritative huff. I peered around the corner to see Becca crouched in a ball, hugging her knees. I rushed to her and got down on my haunches.

"Bec? Are you okay? What happened?" I asked.

Becca's head snapped up at me. Angrily she pushed away the tears that were streaming down her face. "Nothing. Nothing at all. I'm so stupid."

I didn't know how to respond. I'd never seen Becca cry. To be honest, I didn't know she *could* cry, well, there was the day of our first runway show that she'd clearly been crying. "Um, okay," I muttered. "So, the group is going out to that new fondue place on the west side. Should I tell them to go ahead without us?"

"No. I'm fine. Let's go," she said in a huff. She stood and grabbed her bag slinging it over her shoulder defiantly.

CHAPTER 10

You would think that living with, and fucking, a woman for three years would give you some clue about her mood swings. Nope. Not one bit. I'd just found her in a puddle of tears and now she's ready to binge on carbs. Women!

At the restaurant, I watched her carefully. I'd just witnessed the Great Rebecca Campbell, tower of stone and strength, crumble. And here she was, only an hour later, partying hard, and wolfing down cheese dipped everything, as well as knocking back the martinis faster than the waitress could bring them.

The bill was paid and one by one, our friends dropped off, but Becca refused to give up the fight. The last of our friends hanging on was Lisa. Her and Becca started a separate tab. I chose to stick to RC Cola knowing one of us would have to stay sober. I had never been a fan of Lisa. She'd only joined our group last month. She made me nervous. But not in the way you'd think.

A few weeks ago I went home with her, after confirming there weren't any other hot chicks around. Working in my new way of dominating women and making them do all sorts of things before I'd fuck them and leave them satisfied Jack Stevens Style, Lisa took it to another level. I had her on her hands and knees, I was buried balls deep in her and she begged me to spank her. Oh the times I've wanted to whack a girl's ass, and never dared to—here was a chick asking, no— *begging* me to do it.

Not needing another invitation, I brought my hand down and squarely smacked her ass. She lurched, moaned and trembled, her pussy clamping down and milking my cock. She wiggled her ass slightly and I let it rip again, to the same effect. My hand stung slightly, and my cock was getting an incredible milking. I reached up and grabbed a fistful of her fake blonde hair tugging her deeper onto me. Her breathing quickened and we were both beyond aroused.

This was no ordinary fuck. I rammed into her so hard and fast, it was all a blur, and as I came, I spanked her again, hungry for that milking cunt.

When we were done, I dressed quicker than I had in times past. Normally I stayed and cuddled a bit. Not that I was soft, but I was selfish. There was something about touching all that soft skin after a satisfying fuck. But this time, I was scared. The power I felt spanking her, the way she moaned and trembled... I'd never experienced that. And I wanted more. But I didn't do relationships. And I didn't trust Lisa's motives.

"Hey, let's get out of here and have some real fun," Lisa said, winking at me and pulling me out of my memories. Did Lisa know that Becca was gay? Was she suggesting a three-way? There wasn't anything I would have put past that girl.

"What did you have in mind, love?" Becca slurred.

"We should probably turn in," I tried. The pit of my stomach turned knowing that what was in the works would change things forever.

"Nonsense, Jackie..." Becca said, laying it on thick. "Let's go have some fun. Lisa's the captain. Let's vote. All in favor, say yes in, um, Russian. Ready, vote! *Dah!* Aww, sorry Jack-o-lantern, you didn't get your vote in. So, mine is the one that counts."

Becca thumbed out a hundred dollars proclaiming that it should be enough to cover the last few drinks we'd had, and the three of us headed to the curb. Lisa hailed a cab and ushered us inside and, giddy as a school girl, she gave an address to the driver. Ten minutes later we were on a dark street that reeked of bad news. Calmly she paid the driver and we got out. We'd barely closed the taxi door before the driver high-tailed out of there. That couldn't be a good sign.

She wriggled her eyebrows, which didn't match the color of her hair. Calmly, Lisa walked over to a large, heavy, unmarked door and pulled it open. Once inside, we could faintly hear the thump of music. It sounded like a rave party that was the new thing. But those were generally lots of acid and coke and other shit.

"Look, Lisa, we don't do drugs," I said, pulling Becca into my side protectively.

"Neither do I, silly. Like I'm going to ruin my career with cheap blow. But—a warning, this will be a high like none other."

With a confident swagger, Lisa headed in the direction of the driving beat. Becca pulled on me with a fun-loving smile that I couldn't say no to. I didn't want to go, but I knew she was going to with or without me. I listened to the brother in me and chose to accompany her. She'd see that this was bad news and I'd be able to get her back home. We rounded the corner where Lisa waited chatting with a huge man that looked a lot like Lou Ferrigno from *The Incredible Hulk*.

"D, these are my friends, J and B. They're my guests tonight, so be nice."

D nodded gruffly winking at Lisa, who was already dragging Becca toward another door where it was obvious the music was coming from. Lisa opened the door and the music swallowed us whole.

CHAPTER 11

Peering into the dark, I was suddenly pulled forward by Becca and the door closed behind us. After the loud assault of the sound wore off, I became aware of the heavy scent of baby oil and sex. Under the music you could hear disturbing sounds that didn't compute. Snapping sounds. Screaming sounds.

Stepping into the darkness, I noticed we were in a small entry way that sounded like it had padded walls. Small puddles of light were spilling about the room. I willed my eyes to adjust.

"L, darling… how lucky to have you back so soon." A short, round man with a foreign accent stepped up to Lisa and the two exchanged European cheek kisses. "And I see you brought some *friends*," he said in a tone that was too excited, but what got me more was how he checked me out more than Lisa or Becca. At least they were safe, I could fend for myself.

"I have a feeling that these two might be your new regulars. S, this is B and J." Lisa and Becca looked at one another and burst out laughing, and in no time at all they were laughing so hard that tears were rolling down their faces. "Omigod, that is so perfect!" Lisa squealed.

"J, B, It's nice to meet you," *S* said, greeting us. "Please enjoy yourselves. I'm sure that L will fill you in on the rules. She's one of our best clients. And wickedly talented, too," he said, winking at Lisa before bestowing her with another kiss and taking his leave.

Lisa shucked her wrap and took Becca's from her and brought them to a coat check girl that I'd not noticed earlier.

"Locker twelve. Thanks," Lisa bubbled at the girl.

"Come," Lisa urged, wedging herself between Becca and myself and pushing us around the corner. What we encountered after rounding the corner stunned me like nothing before.

And suddenly the snaps and screams made sense. I looked around the large room and felt faint. There was a woman bound and bent over a table, her arms and legs strapped down. A large man with his face covered like he was the Lone Ranger was standing behind her, holding what looked like a hundred thin, black and red leather strips brought together in one handle. He was slapping figure eights across her ass that was pushed in his direction. The look on her face was blissful. He was hitting her ass and she liked it? He suddenly stopped and walked over to the wall. He replaced the leather strappy thing on the wall and selected a riding crop.

"Are you ready?" he asked the trussed girl in a commanding voice.

She slowly nodded her head yes, her eyes still softly closed. She couldn't talk because she was gagged with a leather strap with a ball affixed to it. He brought the riding crop to his left and backhanded the stick across her bare ass. She would have screamed, but the ball shoved in her mouth effectively blocked the sound. The look on her face was unmistakable. It wasn't the face of pain, rather a pre-orgasmic face. I looked at her ass, bright pink, now with a line across her right butt cheek. It was beautiful. My cock started to swell and throb in my pants.

Sex clubs were all over this town. I'd been to a couple like *Plato's Retreat,* a popular swinger's club in the basement of the Ansonia Hotel. Man, the "Mattress Room" was a trip. I stayed away from the gay places, places like *The Playpen* at Times Square and most of the places in the appropriately named Meatpacking District, it just wasn't my scene. I found myself now wondering if Becca had been to any of the gay clubs. But, this place was like *The Vault,* and *Mineshaft.* This was an S&M club. *Holy shit balls!* I'd stayed away from those—er—these places.

"Isn't it beautiful?" Lisa asked her lips millimeters from my ear. "I'm so envious of her right now. My cunt is twitching. Afterward, she's going to get fucked like there's no tomorrow."

The crack of a whip drew my attention to the right. A man stood, shirtless with his back to the center of the room, his arms suspended overhead with a pair of cuffs securing his wrists. Looking more closely, his back had what looked like several cuts on it. Movement to his left drew my attention to a chesty, blonde woman standing about eight feet from him. She was dressed in black, skin tight pants and a matching black bikini top. She raised her hand and the long tail of a whip came down on his back again. The man's body jerked and trembled. I looked away, unable to process how all of this made me feel. I wasn't as appalled as I should have been. My cock grew to a near steel hardness.

Forcing my gaze to the far left, a handsome man sat back on a leather sofa surrounded by three naked women. One was settled in between his legs clearly giving the man great head, while his head was thrown back and he was groaning. Meanwhile the other two were french kissing each other in front of him while his hands gripped harshly at their breasts.

"See something you like?" Lisa asked. "Want Becca and I to get a third girl and do that for you?"

I looked nervously at Becca. She was riveted, chewing on her lower lip. Her hand was on her breast and she was squeezing, and none too lightly. Lisa then leaned over and kissed Becca deeply.

"Come. Let's walk, but no touching. Unless you have permission from the parties involved. And for your information, *you* have my *full* permission," she said, winking at me before leading the way.

In the four corners of the room were beds. The first corner we came upon was a "run of the mill" orgy, if you could call it that. Three men and two women, all fully naked. It reminded me of the "Mattress Room." The sight was enough to have me nearly exploding in my jeans.

A redhead was on her hands and knees with a man standing in front of her. She had his full cock working in and out of her mouth, and she was getting fucked from behind at the same time by another guy who was sucking the tits of this blonde who was getting eaten by this third guy. My dick ached as it pounded in my pants. Staring at the group, I felt more than a little perverted. But when the redhead looked up and locked eyes with me, smiling around the other man's junk, I knew that she wanted me to be watching her.

Lisa tugged on my arm and we followed Becca who was walking in a trance. We headed toward the man who was strung up, being whipped by the severe-looking blonde, walking in front of him. As we did, I saw his cock hanging out of his pants and tied up with leather strings. It was bulging and purple. My cock pulsed with concern, and a little intrigued. As the whip came down on his back again, his cock leapt, mine mimicking the action. Lisa groaned wickedly and we continued our journey around the room.

Next, we came to a bed of women. All women. I couldn't count how many. Some kissing. Some eating pussy while getting eaten. And there were dildos lying all over the bed. How I wanted to climb into that mix of soft flesh and gentle moans and whispers. The snake in my pants was painfully pressing on the zipper of my jeans. My heart was pounding so hard in my chest, it felt like it was bruising. I glanced at Becca. She looked like she might pass out at any moment from panting so hard.

"You could join them, Bec. They wouldn't mind. But Jacks, you'll have to stay put. That's a lady-love-only bed. No salami."

"Could I?" I heard Becca ask, her fingers already working on the buttons down the front of her shirt.

I flew to her side and stopped her right there. "Next time, love. Let's see what else is here." I didn't want her jumping into something while she was so drunk. She must have been really drunk because she nodded numbly in agreement.

"Party pooper," Lisa pouted.

We continued our walk passing a softly lit hallway. "What's down there?" I asked as casually as I could manage.

"Those are private rooms. Not everyone is an exhibitionist. How about you Jack? Would you like to put it all on display? Or are you more private than that?"

The crack of a whip and an unbridled cry came from a door on one side of the hallway. On the other side, we could hear grunts. Manly grunts. Satisfied grunts. Some dude was getting it good. My cock was jealous. All the sounds of sex and dominance engulfed me. I started to sweat. I needed to get laid in the worst way—and soon. I hoped Becca wouldn't pass out as soon as we got back to the apartment.

"The three of us could get a room. Could be fun. Is your palm itchy?" she asked me knowingly.

I wanted a room, but I didn't. I couldn't get involved with Becca in that way. What we had was… Well, I don't know what it was, but I didn't want a threesome with Lisa. I did however find myself wanting to watch Lisa and her go at it. And my hand was experiencing an odd tingling like when I'd spanked Lisa last time. My cock throbbed as it recalled her milking snapper.

I looked over at Becca and, with one glance, I knew she was about to hurl. "Quick, Lisa, she's gonna puke."

Lisa was always cool under pressure, and for once I was grateful. She dashed and picked up a bucket from God knows where for God knows what, and had it in front of Becca just as she began puking her guts up. And with that, our little adventure to the sex club was officially ended.

I swept Becca up in my arms and we swiftly exited, none the wiser to all the couples and groups moaning, writhing, crying and orgasming all around us.

Back in the apartment, I showered Becca, as I'd done a number of times before. Her binge drinking was, sadly, not new, but when she got emotional, she tended to lose it. The emotional aspect fortunately wasn't often. But when it happened, it was ugly.

"Wasn't that crazy?" she asked, half awake as I dried her hair.

"Wasn't what crazy?" I asked. *That guy, Danny, who broke your heart is a not a man, but is a woman who's a bitch? Or the sex club with the leather and whips?*

"That club? Please tell me I didn't imagine it."

"It was a crazy club," I agreed.

"What part did you like the most?"

"Ha! Lemme see. Which did I like the most? I'll have to think about that."

She smiled as I slipped a T-shirt from Barcelona over her head. She snuggled down onto her pillow. "There were so many things I liked. We'll have to try some one day, okay?" she said through a yawn.

"Get some sleep," I said tucking her in.

To say I had a tough time falling asleep that night was an understatement. Yes, I had one ear out for Becca, and all that I thought I knew about her. This new Danny/Dani revelation was only a suspicion, something I'd have to confirm tomorrow. But now, my mind was racing with the whips and shit I'd just witnessed. The sounds of the whips and crops, mixed in with the moans and gasps and layered with the sights of the pink and brown flesh.

Some of the scenes were just like the regular sex clubs. The orgy bed. The sofa where the guy was being serviced by the three women. The bed of women. Those were incredibly hot, but the images most scratching at my mind were those where a person was bound and being whipped.

That girl tied down on the horse, what was she getting out of it? Clearly she liked it, but why? She wasn't able to move, or talk, but her face was absolutely enthralled and at peace. The leather strands smacking her ass, left her cheeks good and pink. I bet it was warm to the touch too. And when the crop was added... She knew it was coming. I knew that a riding crop could hurt. My brother, Kurt, once thought it would be funny to whip me like a horse. It didn't feel sexual at all. It hurt like a mother fucker and left a mark for a week. Why was it different when that girl had it done to her?

The guy who was strung up and getting whipped was the most intriguing to me. What was he getting out of it? He stood and took the whips to his back. I was surprised that there were mostly only markings on his back and that he wasn't bleeding much at all. What I was most curious about was the look on his face when we saw the front of him. He looked pained while waiting for the crack of the whip, but when it came down, he looked purely relieved. And the way his tied up cock reacted had me more confused than all of it.

My cock was rock hard and needed relief. Becca was passed out and therefore unavailable. As I stroked it with my hand, I imagined what it would feel like had my balls been tied up like that guy. What was the point? With my other hand, I closed off my balls as much as I could and I continued to stroke. While normally stroking made my cock hard and I came easily, with my balls shut off, my cock was wickedly hard. And when I couldn't stand it anymore, I released my grip and *mother-fucking-holy-shit!* I came so hard and loud, I was scared I'd woken Becca up.

I cleaned up and checked in on Becca. She was snoring like a lumberjack.

Laying back in bed, I hated Lisa for taking us there, but at the same time, I wanted to ask her to take me back. I needed to see more. I needed to learn more.

CHAPTER 12

The next morning, Becca didn't mention the club, nor did I. I had a feeling she was thinking about it, but I wasn't going to be the one to bring it up. Instead, I quietly served her coffee and toast. Becca was quiet when she was hungover, but this morning she was absolutely melancholy.

We sat quietly, both of our minds turning. Not sure what was going through her mind, but I had so much running through mine I thought I'd explode.

"Becca, can I ask you a question?" I asked quietly.

"You just did," she replied, throwing on an interview ready smile, already trying to deflect what she sensed was coming.

I chewed on my lip and cracked my knuckles which earned me a glare. She hated when I did that. I couldn't help it. I always cracked my knuckles when I was nervous.

"Out with it," she growled.

"Are you… You know…" I let the sentence trail off, not sure which word to use. *Gay. Lesbian. Homosexual.*

"Impossibly beautiful? Outrageously talented? Wickedly smart? Yes. Yes. And *hell yes!*"

"Forget it," I muttered. This was going to go nowhere.

"What, Jackie? Just say it." I gritted my teeth. I had to get her to stop calling me that. "Are you gonna ask your question or what?"

I took a deep breath and let it out in a puff. "Danny. The g—the *person* that broke your heart just before I moved in. Was that short for Danika?"

"What the—? That's how rumors get started. Why would you even ask that?"

"Well, I overheard you and her… talking… It sounded like—"

Becca got up off the sofa and went to the window. She pulled back the curtain and stared silently.

"I'm sorry. I overstepped," I apologized. I got up and went over to her. I was surprised to see tears in her eyes again. Becca never cried, now this was the second time in two days. Critiques, harsh reviews, or being rejected from a job, she was always strong and it didn't seem to bother her.

"I knew it was over. I was just being silly," she whispered. "First love, you know? You never get over it, I guess," she sobbed, turning into my chest and clutching around my waist.

"Gotta say, I never saw this coming," I said, shaking my head.

"You saw what you wanted to see. Classic psychology," she scoffed.

She was always spouting off psychology bits. She had graduated from Columbia not only with a major in English but a minor in psych.

The feel of her sobbing, complete with hiccups, broke my heart for her. "Hey, hey…" I soothed, rubbing her back. "There's someone out there. And she's worthy of being with someone like you." What the fuck? I was talking like a girl. I better find my balls or they're gonna come for my man card.

"It's not easy for people like me. When you're straight, people accept you. Gay? And with this whole HIV/AIDS thing flying all around… Worse, I like both dicks and chicks. Being pulled by two worlds. My parents won't talk to me. They'll accept my fame, but not me. It just hurts so badly and I can't do a thing about it. And I've loved having you as a roommate and the fucking and now—"

"Whoa! Hold your horses," I interrupted. I pushed her back, still holding onto her shoulders, and studied her red, blotchy face. She looked different. Scared. Sad. Lost. "I'm not going anywhere. It's gonna take more than you lookin' for lady love to get rid of me."

"You're just saying that so you don't have to pay rent." She turned from me and went back to her perch on the sofa.

I went over and knelt before her. "Look, Becca. We have a lot in common."

"What… you're gay too?" she asked sarcastically.

"Uh, no. But hey, we both have parents that won't talk to us. We both have the same job that judges us for what we look like, not who we are. And now I learn that we both like women. This is perfect. If I'd known we could have compared chicks on that level we'd have had a whole lot more fun these past few years."

She studied my face for a moment. "You really don't care?"

"No. You're the best friend I've ever had. A friend with benefits. You never demand things from me. You make me feel wanted. I'm the youngest of eight. My whole life was hand-me-downs and leftovers. You and me? Our little family works. I couldn't be happier than hanging with you. But if you want me out of here…"

"NO! God. Jackie, if I'd—"

"Can you please stop calling me that?" I sighed.

"What? Jackie?"

"Yeah. I'm not a chick. It's Jack. Just Jack. Not Jackie. Not Jacks. Not Jack-o-lantern. *Not* Jackass Jack. Just Jack. Although, maybe now I understand why you call me Jackie…"

She slapped my shoulder, "Okay. Just Jack. Or would you prefer J?"

"Oh. My. God. Was that the trippiest scene last night or what?"

Suddenly, the intercom rang. I answered the phone, and the doorman said that Lisa was here checking on Becca. Against my better judgment, I let her up. Becca and I were talking in a way that we never had. I thought she was my best friend before, but we'd just taken things to a whole new level. And I really wanted to hash through what we'd seen last night without Lisa in the way. But it was nice of Lisa to stop by. Besides, maybe I could get the address of that place from her.

Becca went to the bathroom to clean up from her cry just as Lisa tapped on the door. I let her in and offered her a cup of coffee.

"God, yes. Please! How's Becca? Who knew sex could make someone puke, huh?"

She followed me into the kitchen where I poured her a cup of coffee. She picked it up and drank it black. Not sure why, but that surprised me. I figured her for a super sweet and milky coffee drinker.

As we made ourselves comfortable in the living room, Becca came out of the bathroom looking grey, but a little more cheery than before. At least all the snot was cleared off her face.

"Becca, baby. How are you feeling? Hair of the dog, what should I make you?" Lisa asked turning to the bar table.

"Oh, God, Leese. No. Couldn't possibly." Becca picked up her coffee and curled up on the sofa, pulling a cashmere throw around her.

"Well, water at the very least." Lisa ducked into the kitchen and came out with a glass of water and a couple of aspirin.

Becca took them gratefully and sat back.

"So, Lisa. Jack, or *J,* and I were just talking... That place last night. How did you know about it? And clearly you're a regular," Becca started in.

A sly grin spread across Lisa's face. She studied both our faces.

"You liked it, huh?" she asked, leaning closer to me. She pushed her tits together making them nearly spill out of her low cut tank top.

"Hey, I'm a red-blooded guy," I shrugged. Lisa got up and went to sit next to Becca.

"I'm going back tonight, wanna...come?" she asked suggestively.

I saw the look in her eye and that she was hoping we would go as a couple. I didn't want to go with her, I just wanted to go.

CHAPTER 13

B, L and I became club regulars, and soberly after that first visit. For the first couple of weeks we just watched, taking it all in, absorbing the rules, and getting to know who was who. There were all kinds there. Most were committed partners, some were swingers, others were flings. Lisa was all over the place. She had some Masters she'd go back to time and again for a load of debasement. She allowed herself to be collared and lead around on a leash while she crawled on her hands and knees. Sometimes she was a full-on dominatrix and giving no mercy to the men she was whipping. She was what was referred to as a Switch, sometimes a Domme, sometimes a submissive.

Becca took cues from Lisa. She enjoyed being controlled, but seemed most comfortable as a Domme. She liked being the one in charge. It suited her. Typically on modeling jobs, she behaved as if she was the one in control, but it was mostly a ruse and she knew it. She wasn't in charge, but they tried to make her feel that way. At the club, when she was with the women, she was absolutely in charge. It was a beautiful thing to watch. Especially the way she threw a whip.

She'd met this one submissive in the club, a cute little redhead called R. She was adorable, but never gave me the time of day. In the club, the two were considered an unbreakable item, but only at the club. When I asked Becca about her relationship with R, she said, "Just at the club. I'm not getting my heart broken again."

I was a 'once-and-done' kind of guy, in the club and out. Out of the club, I'd been getting it on with groupies that followed us models around. They were using me, hoping they'd be photographed and discovered. They were using me, and I was using them. I'd fuck chicks from the club, we'd have fun then go our separate ways. Occasionally, one would ask for my number, or give me hers. I never called them, and I never gave out my number. Interestingly, it didn't really bother but a couple of them. There were a few models I connected with, and we'd see each other for a month or so, but their egos got in the way, and after a couple fucks with them, they weren't worth the effort. They were always too concerned with how they looked, or they were out of their minds from blow, or drunk, or strung out from too many laxatives.

After a few months, Becca and I started attending classes, seminars and workshops at the club. We learned about floggers, crops and whips. Bondage techniques. Punishment versus play. Subspace and aftercare. It was as if my eyes had been opened to something that finally made sense. In *this* world there was order. No exceptions. You followed rules and suffered the consequences if you stepped out of line. There was play time, but that was also governed by a set of rules. In the world of modeling, if you didn't perform, you might lose that gig, but someone else was asking for you. When dating as a model, the girls always came back even if you didn't want them to. Back in Colorado, if I stepped out of line, I was either publicly humiliated like what Jenny had done to me by labeling me to everyone we knew, or were like my parents who just ignored me and wrote me off.

We learned a lot of crazy shit with Master N as our mentor. Mental and physical play. Light stuff like bondage and blindfolds, and more intense shit like using canes and whips. The first time I had a whip training class I remember being both excited and scared. After watching the Domme crack the long strand of leather at the guy from that first night, it was the one aspect of the club that stuck with me. The first time I threw the six-foot kangaroo hide bullwhip, the tail came back and snapped me in the face. *Fuck!* Not only did it hurt like a bitch, but I had a photo shoot in three days.

"It's more than slinging a whip, J. You need to own it. Right now, you own shit. It's very easy, you need to stop overworking it," Master N said. And for the next few weeks we worked on my technique until my arms ached and I had quite a collection of cuts from mis-throws. Eventually I was able to throw with impressive accuracy. I wasn't as good as Becca. She was a natural.

Watching B handle the whip was a thing of beauty. She quickly worked her way up to a nine-foot whip. But it wasn't just her skill. She was transformed when she took control. It was the way she wanted to appear on the sets of photo shoots.

When Master N felt I was ready to finally start using the skills I'd been learning in the workshops in the club, he introduced me to A. She was perfect. I'd seen her around the club many times. We'd shared glances, but never time.

I was in a private room. Master N accompanied me, as was protocol for a novice using tools for the first time. I looked around the modest space that was illuminated with a soft, warm lighting. The walls were painted a warm brown, and along the far wall was a bureau that housed all sorts of implements. Blindfolds. Restraints ranging from cuffs, both metal and leather, to cuffs on spreaders. Crops. Coiled whips. New packages with items like ball gags, nipple clamps, dildos of all sizes, and anal beads and plugs. There was a large bed with crisp white sheets.

A, a petite brunette with her hair pulled back in a severe pony tail that hung neatly down her back to her waist, walked into the room completely naked. After she closed the door, she clasped her hands behind her back and knelt before me, her proud breasts pushed forward. She knew her place. Master N watched silently as I shrugged my shirt off and handed it to A.

"Hang up my shirt, please, and return."

Without haste, the girl leapt up and collected my shirt. She hung it with care on the wall, then returned to her kneeling position in front of me. I stood stunned.

"Are you here for punishment or play?" I asked.

"Play, Sir," she replied, a smile spreading across her face as she kept her eyes downcast. I watched her chest heave as her excitement grew. I had my own growing response.

"Devices?"

Her breath increased. "Flogger, and then crop please, Sir." Her voice wavered with excitement.

"How many?"

She bit her lip and eyed me carefully. "Four," her voice rang confidently.

"Standing or horse?" I offered, my own voice growing strained with anticipation.

"I prefer to stand please, Sir."

I commanded her to stand and place her hands on the wall. She did so obediently, while wagging her perfect derrière as she moved to the wall. I took the flogger from the collection in the room and proceeded to warm her skin. Exercising the care and technique I'd learned from Master N and under his watchful eye, I covered her backside from her shoulder blades down her back to the backs of her thighs, careful to avoid her lower back and kidney area so I wouldn't cause any life threatening damage. The pinking of her skin combined with her gentle mews drove me insane. After forty or so strokes she was quietly humming, an indication that she was in subspace.

I returned the flogger and picked up the crop. I smacked it into the palm of my hand, the sting centering my own growing need. When she heard the sound, she moaned.

"Are you ready for your first strike?" I asked.

"Sir, I am," she breathed.

"Count." Slowly she nodded and I saw her fingers flex on the wall as she readied herself.

I brought the crop onto her right cheek. She clenched her ass and gripped the wall. "One," she sighed. I watched as a pink stripe rose to the surface of her butt cheek. I checked her face. She looked perfect. She looked like she was in heaven.

Three more pops and her count was over. I dropped the cane and pulled her into my lap. Sensing the tool play was over, Master N stepped out quietly. She was still writhing.

"You did great, A."

"Thank you, Sir. Your technique is well trained, Sir." She sighed, her head dropping onto my chest.

I ran my hand up over her thighs and waist. She jutted her hips into me sending me a message that she wanted play to change to sex. I brought my hand up between her thighs and found that she was soaking wet. Slipping in a finger, then two, and finally three, I swiftly pumped her to an orgasm. It intrigued me that I'd more or less hurt her, yet she was incredibly turned on by it. Yes, we had an understanding and rules. Takes all kinds I guess. I knew that the power and being in control turned me on in indescribable ways.

After she came down from my fingering her, she slid off of my lap and bent over me, pulling my dick out of my Adidas pants. She took me in her mouth and in one swift motion, the head of my cock was down her throat, and my pubes were pushed up against her face. *What a sight!* She expertly went at me teasing and sucking. She knew what she was doing. I loved this club. Top quality. She had a grip constricting me at the top of my balls, like that guy who had the strap around his cock. I felt myself grow to an unimaginable hardness. I was like fucking steel. It burned, yet was incredible.

I was at my end, gripping the back of her head, and pounding my hips into her face. I was growling like a caged animal. She released her grip on my sac and I exploded with the force of a volcano. The way A had controlled that orgasm rocked my world.

CHAPTER 14

The first time I was under the control of a Master, I was hooked. I had felt the bite of the whip as a part of training, not to mention the dozens of shitty throws that had the business end of the whip come back at me.

It had been a nightmare of a week with a location shoot that was a disaster. Bad weather conditions, long hours, crappy food, a godawful room that I had to share with this other guy, Rick, who was a total slob, and there was this Amanda, this model who'd been trying to get me into bed for a while. We fucked, but as I predicted, she was like a dead fish in bed. She got more than a little scared when I slipped in to Dom mode with her and I was probably a little more harsh than I should have been, but she won't be barking up this tree again. Good enough. I didn't do repeats. *Love 'Em and Leave 'Em* as the Kiss song went.

I was sitting at the bar considering quitting the modeling scene all together, when a gorgeous, buxom blonde with fierce green eyes approached me. I recognized her as the woman who was whipping the man my first visit to the club. She introduced herself as Mistress C, ordered a Macallan, and asked if I'd been a good boy or bad boy that week. It was a tired pick up line in this place, but instantly, the way I'd treated Amanda came to mind.

"You seem upset," she pushed when I didn't answer.

"Tough week at work, you could say." I threw back the rest of my Jack Daniels on the rocks and prayed that the burn would erase the feelings.

"Can I get you another?" she asked.

I nodded. The bartender pulled down the bottle of Jack. Mistress C stopped him and tapped the glass in front of her. The bartender put the

Jack back and grabbled the bottle of Macallan and a fresh glass, no ice, and slid it in front of me.

"For what was done to you, or for what you did?" she asked raising a brow, taking a sip of the drink in front of her. I watched as she savored the brown liquid. I took a sip of the same and appreciated the smoother quality.

"Does it matter?" I asked turning to her.

"Sure. I can help you work it out, but you have to know what side you're on."

I thought about that for a moment. You could say it was both.

As far as what was done to me, well, it was all the demands that are put on you as a model. Where to be, what time to be there, how to stand, how to look, hours of being primped—which I hated beyond belief, then the standing around while the 'real talent'—the girl—was prepped, and not to mention how much Amanda liked to brag about her paycheck. I was never considered smart in school. Getting a C+ was a big deal for me. But no calculators were needed to figure out that she was getting paid fifty thousand dollars more than I was getting.

As far as what I'd done, it was the way I'd treated said model. She said she was consenting. I didn't mark her or anything, but I got a wicked thrill out of controlling her. Blindfolding her. Tying her to the bed. Withholding her orgasms from her. Making her swallow. The next day she avoided me, which was actually the result I wanted, but she looked more scared than upset. I could have apologized, but what was the point.

"And how does being at the end of your whip help me?"

"If you're being lashed for something you've done, giving in to the control of someone else can be freeing. If it's for something done to you, it can release the anger you're probably harboring. For men, especially powerful men like you, it's quite liberating."

I considered what she'd said. Maybe there was something to her theory.

I eyed her suspiciously. "Let's go, then."

"So, are you receiving a punishment for what you did? Or are you taking a lashing to release the stress?"

"Does it matter?" I asked, narrowing my eyes at her.

"No. Not to me."

"Are we gonna do this or what?" I asked, growing impatient.

She swallowed more of her Scotch then stood.

"First time. Horse," she said, pointing to the black, leather clad horse in the center of the room.

"The center of the room? Hell no. This is bull shit." I yanked out my wallet and threw a twenty dollar bill on the bar and started to walk away.

"Fine. Let it fester," her cold voice sang from behind me.

I stopped and *felt* the words echo in my brain. I knew she was right. It *would* fester. It would grow. I would try and numb the ache with Coors, Jack and Stoli. I knew that the numb from the booze would only last the night. Maybe Becca and I would try and fuck it out. This had been the cycle. For years. When I felt out of control, or had taken too much control, I felt like shit. I drank like mad. Days would pass until I felt better. Then, as soon as I was on set, or having my way with a chick, the feeling would come back.

"Fuck! Fine!"

"No!" she barked and stood. Her breath brushed on my neck. "Not fine. You commit, or we don't do this."

I looked toward the horse. There, lying willingly, no binds to hold her, no blindfold or gag, was a pale redhead. Another woman stood behind her; a Domme. She wasn't using a traditional flogger, she was using a ballchain cat.

The sub's face was tear streaked, yet she looked to be in heaven. At peace. Relieved. I wanted that peace.

I turned and I searched Mistress C's green eyes. There was confidence. There was authority. There was … hope. I cocked an eyebrow at her, accepting her challenge and started to unbutton my shirt.

"I need this. I want this," I whispered, nodding slightly.

A tiny smile appeared on her face. A curt nod. I had my permission.

I strode to the horse where the pale thing lay in her private nirvana. I unbuttoned my shirt and draped it on a coat hook. I felt several eyes on me. Did they recognize me? I knew that the general understanding here was anonymity, but I couldn't help but wonder if someone would recognize me. I felt like I was on the set of my first photo shoot. Like all eyes were on me and judging.

I didn't see the redhead leave. I didn't see Mistress C appear next to me. But suddenly the redhead was gone and the horse was free. Mistress C extended her hand for me to take my position on the horse. I felt odd. I looked at her. The look in her eyes set all my fears aside. I drew from her confidence.

Standing in front of the horse, I eyed it and took a deep breath. As I settled my body on the cool leather, she asked with her mouth brushing on my ear, "Cuffs?"

I took a few more breaths and considered the choice. Tied down? Or here on my free will? I wanted both. But I knew what I needed. "Cuffs." I needed to know I had committed.

Swiftly, Mistress C cuffed my wrists and ankles. I lay there knowing what to expect. I had the training. I tried to steady my breath in preparation for the flogger. I knew that she would bring me to subspace first. Then the punishment. I started to panic when I realized we hadn't agreed on a number of lashes. That was supposed to have happened first. Part of the establishment phase. I didn't have that. She hadn't asked.

But then, the first of the falls came across my back. The sting was sharp. It was reassuring. Instantly I felt a calm fall over me. A second, then a third cascade of leather strands caressed my back. Again and again. With each crashing, I gave in. I gave up my struggles. The frustrations from the job. The annoyances of the women who wanted to be with me because I was a model, not because I was me. The shame for needing to demonstrate control over those women. The warmth that covered my back was comforting and at the same time, oddly erotic. I nearly felt drunk.

"Are you ready?" I heard Mistress C say. Her voice echoed in my head slightly. I heard her clearly enough, but it was distant. *So this is subspace,* I thought. I nodded, slow and numb. I needed more.

"Say it. I cannot go further."

My mind searched for the rules. "Yes, Mistress. More, please."

A moment or four passed. *Whoop-tsch!* The warmth that hit my back was initially a tiny spot. Then that heat radiated. And with the growth of the whip's bite, I felt things—bad things—surface under my skin.

It wasn't pain. It wasn't agony. It was etherial. It felt like it was happening to someone else. Perhaps I was watching.

Whoop-tsch! This second crack opened the space. I felt anger bubble and surface.

Whoop-tsch! A third crack. Shame. My heart ached. A soup of emotion swirled under my flesh.

There were several more; I'd lost count. As for the whip, I don't know if I heard the crack before it hit, *as* it hit or *after* it hit. But as each crack shouted, my head and heart opened and let go.

Whoop-tsch! This last crack was harsher. It opened something. A giant *whoosh* of air left my lungs. I felt it was done. My body collapsed. I relaxed. I was spent.

The episode shocked me some. It reminded me of running or working out… at first it's uncomfortable, but you enjoy the survival, and you want to push yourself. Like that runner's high, endorphins flooding your senses. The edge between pain and pleasure was so blurry.

Like an angel from the unknown, my body was blanketed with something, my wrists and ankles were released. My arms were guided into sleeves. I was pulled back and my feet found the floor. I tried to stand, but found that I was in a stupor. Mistress C was suddenly under my right arm and she helped me … away… to someplace dark and warm.

I was laid down on a soft surface… a bed? A sofa? I felt a pair of hands snake under my shirt. A cooling moisture was rubbed in methodically. I imagined that each area of pain on my back was a hole. And those holes let the bad feelings that I had all trapped inside of me escape. And, as those pains were being eased away with the lotion, the holes were being closed. I relaxed into the touch.

"How are you feeling?" a soft voice fell on me.

"Good. Better," I breathed. "Thank you."

A last touch on my skin and the hand disappeared. I heard a door close. Silence hugged me. I relaxed fully. And slept peacefully.

Watching Jack under the whip of Mistress C was a sight. I admired how she wielded a whip. Always with respect and freakish accuracy. And Jack. My darling Jack… He was so very stoic. Took each bite bravely, contemplating it and giving into it. I watched the pain and anguish of the past years surface and release.

Just last night we talked about me using a whip on him. We had been drinking. He asked me to do it. He'd had a tough trip. He said he'd spoken to some subs he'd been with who told him that the bite of the whip could release the stress and anger and frustration. I refused because I had been drinking. One of the first rules of Dominance was to not exert under the influence. It was a good rule for me. I enjoyed exerting my Domme tendencies more than the drink, so I found myself drinking less and less so I could morally take the handle of a whip.

As Mistress C helped Jack off of the horse, I saw a new man. Jack was still handsome and proud, but now he seemed to have a new peace. Mistress C took him to a room where she would deliver the after care. Too bad she wasn't going to fuck him after the lashing—did Jack know that she was lesbian?

CHAPTER 15

March 1986

The next couple of years brought some changes.

I finally decided to get my own place. Found a reasonable condo on East Fifty-first Street. It was a shit hole given that men didn't earn a fraction of what women did, even if I was working for some of the biggest names in fashion, but it was my shit hole.

Becca and I continued to be the best of friends. If I wasn't crashing at her place, she was crashing at mine. We continued to work, but as we both aged, work became more and more difficult to get. Becca continued to see R, or Rita, but it wasn't exclusive. Becca still kept her at arms length. I continued to have random, domineering sex with whoever was willing. But I stayed away from tapping into the modeling pool to indulge my new found preferences in the bedroom.

Becca, Lisa and I continued to visit the club, but Becca and I would also practice at home. Now we weren't just banging each other for release. We would paddle, or whip each other...then fuck. It was still not an emotional thing for either of us. Just a release.

Our "sessions," as we called them, became a routine. If one of us felt like we needed a session, we'd kneel in the middle of a room. The other person would see it and start firing questions. Asking if the kneeler had been bad, to which degree of badness, and what punishment they wanted and how much. Not exactly a conventional D/s relationship, but it worked for us. Most of the time we'd make shit up, but sometimes we were brutally honest. Becca would bring up sad things from growing up with her overbearing parents and how she felt inadequate because of it. She'd ask for a few lashes to let the darkness out. I would sometimes be overcome with sadness, because the women I was with were only with me for my 'celebrity' status. I felt dirty and ashamed, and I would need a bite to feel *something….anything…* because too often, I had stopped feeling. In the privacy of our homes, the release felt so much greater than the release from a whipping at the club. And to receive aftercare in the arms of a true friend was far more healing.

The slowing career was bothersome. It was all I knew. A future without this job was scary. I was getting gigs, sure. And they were great, especially the after parties, but the runway had pretty much stopped for me. As a 24 year old, I couldn't compete with the new 16 year old men coming onboard. I was still under contract for big names, and I prided myself on being the exemplary model on set. It was my strength. I was on time, courteous, and took direction—and was not a diva, like some of these new kids coming into the business.

William and I continued to work on my career, and he seemed to respect all that I did for his company. That said, he was ready to take things to a higher level of competition, and asked me if I wanted to work for him in other ways, like scouting. It was an interesting proposition. I figured I didn't have anything to lose, and only everything to gain, so I started scouting for William and helped bring in new talent. I learned a lot, like it takes many years to gain a foothold in this business of running a modeling agency. Many companies are never widely known, and are small boutique operations. That's how WMW Models, Inc. had been. Now William wanted to go nationwide, and eventually global. My contracts with the big products helped him get to that status where he could finally consider it. William and I were a great pair, and his company grew stronger and stronger. I kept working, but not like I had when I was younger.

In the spring of 1990, my thoughts turned to college. It was why I had gotten into the whole modeling thing anyway. So, even though I was twenty-fucking-nine years old, I collected information from NYU, Columbia, and Fordham. I was hoping that while my grades in high school were nothing to boast about, perhaps my career days as both a model, and helping to build a (now global) modeling agency, would carry some weight.

One night, while we were both in town and hanging at my place, Becca and I had a blast pouring over the catalogs and imagining ourselves in a variety of professions, post modeling career. I had no idea what degree to get, or what I would do with the degree once I'd earned it.

"A chemist! It's perfect for you, Becs. You're always mixing up drinks, now you mix up real chemicals!"

"Shut up!" She pushed back. "Thirty-five year old women do not go back to school. Well, they do, but not this one. Anyway, I already have my English degree. But I *would* do better at chemistry than you would do in business school," she snorted, pushing a catalog in my direction.

"I'd run a kick-ass business!"

"Right. Doing what?" she mused.

"I dunno. Maybe I'll open my *own* modeling company. A boutique agency. I'll focus on male models."

"You'll go broke in a week. You know better than I that men bring in shit checks. Twenty percent of nearly nothing isn't even worth the effort. You wouldn't have a New York address, that's for sure. You'd be back in Hoboken." We both collapsed into laughter, remembering my days when I'd first moved out here.

When we'd calmed down, she pulled the business catalog back to her view.

"So, are you quitting modeling?" she asked hesitantly. Her career had grown to near stand-still, but she stayed involved with pet charities. Becca was one smart cookie and had done a terrific job of saving her money. She owned her condo outright, and lived on the interest her savings provided. It was as if she'd gone to college to study Business, not English.

"No, I still have another couple years on contracts, unless they cut me loose." I muttered. It felt like only time.

"They wouldn't do that. Your face is the link to those hot jeans and super sexy cologne. Times Square still isn't over your underwear billboard."

"You're only as good as your last gig, though, right? These young kids coming on... I can't compete."

"You don't have to. You are your own brand. You're Jack Stevens. I think you'd do all right," she said with a straight face. "I can see it now," she mused, looking off into the distance. "Stevens Modeling Agency."

"You think? Hey! You could work for me. I'd be lost without you."

"Ooo! Can I be your secretary?"

"Sure. I wouldn't trust any one else. We'll call it… *Becks*. Becca and Jack's."

"We'd be unstoppable."

"The problem is that I'm a dunce bucket and could never get into any of these schools. Not to mention, I'm nearly over the hill. I should look into a community college instead."

"Nonsense. Twenty-nine is nothing! Besides, what's celebrity and experience if you can't use it?"

"I'm not a household name like you, Becs," I grimaced. "No one knows Jack Stevens."

"Oh, they may not know your name, but they know your face—and those abs."

"What? These?" I pulled up my shirt and flexed my six-pack. Becca just rolled her eyes at me and shook her head.

We sat just looking at one another. That's the thing about a best friend. Sometimes you don't have to say anything. It was that way with Becs and me.

"So, if you're gonna grow up and go to college, are you also going to get serious about a girl?"

"I'll get serious about a girl if you do," I challenged. She and Rita, were still as tight as ever, even if she wouldn't let Rita move in.

"Ha! Been there, done that. I won't survive it again if I do. But at least I tried. I don't believe you've even tried."

J ack would make an amazing boyfriend, or husband. Caring. Smart. Handsome as hell. Would she mind the relationship Jack and I have?

And as for me getting serious... Rita, dear, sweet Rita. She's the best. And I trust her. I do... And—I love her. Maybe I should get "serious" about her. If we got "serious" would she let me keep Jack? Would she break my heart?

CHAPTER 16

Well, Becca was right and I was easily accepted to both NYU and Columbia. Guess my ten years modeling, plus working for William and the status of his business, along with his letter of recommendation, and knowing William, he probably sent a donation… it all paid off. *Mental note: Repay the favor.*

I chose Columbia because they responded to my application first. Imagine my surprise when I'd gotten accepted into NYU, too. I registered for classes and was genuinely excited about school, which was hilarious because I'd always hated school.

I was in my second semester at Columbia when I met Kari. We were both in Psychology 101. She was a pre-law major. Beautiful with long brown hair, large hazel eyes, and olive toned skin. Shy. She had this laugh that was definitely one of a kind, a melodious quality and light. And, she was incredibly smart, even if she didn't know who I was. She had no idea I was a model. And maybe that was the appeal. She was with me because of me, not my celebrity status.

Kari was so different, reserved, even more than the girls I'd ever gone out with back in high school. Her mother was an elementary school teacher, and her father, a criminal lawyer. Kari was shy about public displays of affection and sex talk. Anything with an innuendo and she was blushing. I found that aspect about her rather endearing. Cute, even. Almost like when I was back in high school. Dating a virgin. I think she still had her V-card, I was pretty sure she did. I didn't have the courage to ask, and she wouldn't come right out and say.

I had high hopes when I took her out to dinner on Valentines Day, but she only let me get to "second base." Her words, not mine. She was barely out of high school herself; nineteen years old. A full ten years younger than me. I'd never thought of dating someone so young before. I don't know if Kari knew how old I was, and I didn't tell her. I didn't really look my age. A benefit of working in an industry with so much focus on looks, I'd always taken good care of my skin, therefore, I looked pretty young. I found the age difference between Kari and me to be comforting in a weird way. Like I was her protector.

Becca's challenge about getting serious about a girl rang in my head when Kari and I first started seeing each other. So taking the relationship seriously, I stopped seeing other women. It took a ridiculous amount of control and I was convinced I was going to develop some horrible disease. One doesn't simply go from four to seven fucks a week, to just his hand, which I was now all too familiar with. I even stopped sleeping with Becca, besides—I was hoping she'd get serious about Rita. But something about being with Kari made it worth it. She made me want to be an upstanding guy. I didn't even feel the need to dominate her, although the thought of turning her olive-toned skin a deep pink crossed my mind more times than I cared to admit.

When we'd go out, she wasn't coming on to me, or bragging about her own achievements. Instead, I took her to dinner, or some touristy site, I even took her skating at Rockefeller Center. I let her drag me shopping, and to the State Supreme Court, and French films in quirky little theaters. I thought she was trying to wind me up with a sexy film, but no. She just liked French and spoke it fluently. We had discussions about the president, about the economy, about what we wanted to do with our degrees. She was planning on using her law degree in the corporate setting, but hadn't pinned down exactly how. I lied and told her I didn't know what I wanted to use my business degree for. We joked that she would come work for whatever business I was going to run. We had real discussions. Real fun. And a real connection. Even if I wasn't completely honest about who Jack Stevens was—a horny, dominant, 'old man' who, by the way, was a model.

Things were going really well. In fact, we had plans for her birthday in late March that involved a hotel. I couldn't believe it when she agreed. I booked a great room at the Waldorf. But before we got to that hotel, she learned of my career, and got a little weird on me. Started pulling away.

We were headed to see the musical *Cats!* It happened to be a nice, mid-March evening, so after taking the 1 Train to Penn Station, we decided to walk to the Winter Garden Theatre. We were walking up Seventh Avenue in Times Square when she looked up and froze. I turned to see what she was looking at. And there it was. A *GUESS!* jeans billboard. I hadn't realized the billboard was up. I'd done those shots nearly eight months back. I looked good. The model with me, Claudia, also in the shot, looked incredible and was hanging on me.

"Is that *you?*" Kari asked, almost breathless.

I ran my hand through my thick, black hair, suddenly embarrassed. I don't know why her reaction set me on my heels that way. Normally, I'd puff my chest and be all '*Yup! Don't I look awesome?*' but the expression on her face told me that such a reply would be bad. "Yeah," I muttered.

"And is that—"

"Claudia Schiffer. Yeah. Super nice. You'd like her a lot."

"Wow. Um. Okay. I need to sit down for a moment."

I whisked her into a nearby coffee shop. It wasn't a nice one, but not much in Times Square was really nice. I hope they clean this place up. I've heard all sorts of stories about how great it used to be.

I got her a coffee with her four sugars, shuddering—how she drank that stuff with so much sugar, I would never know. I sat down across from her and looked at her. She looked white as a ghost.

"So, you're a... model?" I nodded. "Now I understand the looks from the other girls in class. They all stare at you, you know. And they glare at me since we started seeing each other," she said, blowing into her paper cup.

I nodded. I'd seen how the girls stare. I was used to it. But something about Kari's soft mannerisms and terrific smile drew me in. She was so different than the models, and wanna-bes, and groupies I was used to. She wasn't brash. She wasn't arrogant. She needed protection. Of course, Becca's challenge was ringing in my ears, too.

"Look," I started. "I chose you."

"But why? I'm not as pretty as those other girls."

"You're way prettier. They all need hair crimpers and layers of makeup to even come close to your beauty. And you have a beauty they will never have. You're kind and sweet and smart. I'm with you because I want to be with you."

She swallowed and searched my face. But the look on her face told me that she didn't believe a word of it.

"Kar—I'm a model. Not an actor. I'm serious here."

She licked her lips. Her gorgeous, soft, pink lips. Her large hazel eyes blinked a few times, then she nodded. I stood and held out my hand. She took it. Quietly we walked to the theatre. We enjoyed the show. I enjoyed it a lot more than I thought I would. But something from that point on with Kari was different. I felt her pull away.

A couple of weeks after Kari's discovery of my job, and two nights before we were going to be heading to the Waldorf, I went looking for Kari in the library in her favorite corner on the horrible orange sofa. I nearly flipped my lid when she was sitting with another guy. A blonde surfer type. I stood and watched them, disbelieving and hoping I was misinterpreting something. This guy had his arm draped around Kari. And he was saying something low, and she giggled. My girl! My blood boiled. I couldn't hear a thing. He was dragging his finger, his fucking fat handed fingers, up and down her arm. Kari's eye flitted to the side to see his hand.

"Get your fucking hands off of her!" I shouted.

Kari looked up at me surprised, and … guilty? She paled to as white as a ghost and looked completely uncomfortable. The guy just smirked at me, and pulled Kari closer to him.

Something in me unhinged completely. She was mine to protect, and protect her I would. And maybe it was that I was at three months of no sex, and two days from gettin' some.

I charged in, grabbed the dirt bag off the sofa by his Izod shirt and decked him in the face—rancher style. I was sure I broke his nose as the blood spewed from his face while he laid sprawled out on the ground. In an instant we were surrounded by students.

"What the fuck, dude!" he said, making his way to his feet.

"I'm no 'dude.' I'm your worst nightmare," I growled stepping into him. "Touch my girl again and you're a fucking dead man!" I spat.

The guy was as dumb as a box of rocks because what he said next couldn't have been more wrong. He leaned into my face, blood still dripping from his nose, and spat back, "She's not a possession, asshole. She can see whoever she wants. And right now, she's choosing to be with me."

I started to punch the shit out of him to the cheering crowds. Or were they telling me to back off? I couldn't tell. All I knew was this guy thought he had any territory over my girl. And Surfer Dude didn't get one swing in. Wimp.

Long story short, I found myself locked up a jail cell with a swollen hand and surrounded by a dozen diseased dirtbags. I was informed that the Surfer Dude ended up in the hospital and that both he and the University were pressing charges. After Becca bailed me out, I quickly explained all that had happened and made a beeline to Kari's place to apologize, stopping only to pick up two dozen long-stemmed roses. She refused to answer the door. I sat there the whole night until an officer came and told me I had to leave or I'd be locked up again. So I left the flowers and looked forward to seeing her in class the next day.

The next day at school was brutal. Upon my arrival at campus, I was summoned to the dean of the department to discuss the whole incident. I was on probation. One more slip up and I'd be out. When I showed up to psych class, her seat was, and remained, empty. I chalked it up, convincing myself that she was simply ill that day. I hung around after class to talk to Professor Michaels. I asked for a second set of the handouts from the day so I could get them to Kari, but she informed me Kari had transferred to another class. When I got home, I found an official envelope with an "Order of Protection," otherwise known as a restraining order, filed by Kari keeping me away from her.

I called Becca and asked her to meet me at my place. When she got there, I quietly handed her the nine-foot, kangaroo-hide long tail. I tossed off my shirt, dropped to my knees, and asked her to give me twenty-five lashes. She didn't ask any questions. She didn't have to.

Becca stayed with me for two days nursing my skin... and my heart.

The next semester, Kari transferred to Yale. That did it for me. I wasn't meant to have one woman. I wasn't meant to be a part of a couple. I resolved to become a confirmed bachelor and enjoy my domineering kinks, no strings attached.

CHAPTER 17

May 1996

Making it through an Ivy League Business school is fucking hard. A shit load of fucking hard work. And maintaining a successful modeling career and working for a modeling company, all while attending classes, writing papers, working on projects—both independent and group projects—is fucking near impossible. But I did it. Took me six years. But I did it.

My sex life suffered some, especially with New York trying to clean up its act. All the sex clubs were shutting down, including "ours," but Becca kept my emotions in check and she helped me hone my skills with the whip. We both would give each other sessions whenever we needed it for emotional release but because we were both after women, the sex was still just a release not a connection, although I had a sneaking suspicion that things with Becca and Rita were more and more exclusive as time went on. The women I bedded ranged from those saying they could handle being a submissive but really couldn't, to women who were so submissive they were boring. That said, I had school to keep me occupied and Becca to give me my punishment when I'd crossed the line with girls.

Graduating from the Columbia School of Business was a high point for me. Getting Cs in high school was an achievement back in Colorado, so graduating from college, especially an Ivy League, was a feat for sure. And that I was the first Stevens from the Charter Oaks, Colorado Stevenses to go to college was even more amazing. I invited my whole family to the convocation. I hoped everyone would come. I even offered to pay for their trip and stay. Only David, my oldest brother, Mike, Paul, Sharon and Laura came to watch me receive my diploma.

Mary and Patrick didn't come because they were managing the ranch, and Mary was due to have her fourth baby any day now. David said that Dad, at eighty-two, was dealing with some health issues, and couldn't come. I was certain that his issue wasn't health related, rather how I'd gotten the money to pay for college. Laura confirmed that suspicion when she spilled that she overheard him talking to Mom saying he wouldn't be surprised if I'd bought my diploma rather than earned it. He wouldn't even try to understand that modeling wasn't all naked women and sex, although there was plenty of that. (If he only knew!) I offered to help with medical expenses but Mike said that the old man would hear nothing of it, again saying Dad called it "sin money". Mom, who was now seventy-one, cried tears of joy when she heard that I'd finished college, but didn't come to my graduation. Instead she stood next to her husband's side and supported his point of view, that my success was a result of sin.

The plan immediately after graduation was to dive in and start my own company, with Becca as a partner, but she wanted nothing to do with the major operations. She just wanted to be the secretary, and would put in her two cents if I asked for it.

By September, JSS Modeling, Inc. had opened its tiny door and after a year, we had five readily marketable models on the roster. We decided to try it my way, using only male models. William retired and sent me two of his best boys. It felt great to realize my dream, a dream I never knew was in me. It was going slowly, but it was going. Becca wasn't willing to be more than a silent sort of partner, except when I was banging her—yeah, I still made her scream. I'd heard her scream louder with Rita and it was always a challenge I kept in the back of my mind that I wanted to make Becca scream louder with me than Rita, but to date, I'd not been able to realize that challenge. The more I thought about it, the more I thought Becca was actually a lesbian, not bi.

Struggling with my own company, I started to admire William more and more. It's hard to branch out on your own, and when William started, he had experience and a background of managing models. Now that I was the one managing models, I felt that when I went to the table to pitch, those in charge of casting were thinking I was a joke. I'd worked with many of them as a model, and they didn't know what to make of me as a businessman.

I couldn't believe that the girls kept coming. Yeah, most were out for getting their own careers jump-started, but were more than willing to give me jollies. And I tended to only date women ten years younger than me. Gave the tabloids and industry rags some good gossip, but I didn't care.

A few years into my business's life, Becca convinced me to bring on a few chicks to 'pay the bills.' She was right. She always was. And with those few women, we started to gain a serious foothold in the market-place.

In 2000, I was still trying to send my family the random check to help the ranch stay afloat. And every check I sent was returned. I was near desperate to find a way to help, and in talking with a fellow business school graduate from Columbia came up with a plan. There was a new push on the market place seeking organic beef. Dad ran his ranch 'the way God intended' and never considered growth hormone, blanket antibiotics, or restricted herding with his livestock. His herds enjoyed free range and grazing of untreated fields. I sought out restaurants that used certified organic beef, and convinced a few of these restaurants to simply reach out to the Stevens Ranch and see if they could strike a deal. Bingo! Dad took the contracts and was proud that his beef had made its way into the high-end restaurant scene in New York City. Not saying it wouldn't have happened without my secret intervention, but my hand in the orchestration *was* the key in this case. Soon, four restaurants were serving Stevens Beef.

My business also continued to grow until 9/11 hit, and we were knocked back, nearly to square one. I'd lost more than a few trusted friends that day. It was a tough pill to swallow, but I had to push on. I couldn't 'let the terrorists win.' By 2005, we were back to where we'd been prior to the attack on the World Trade Center Buildings. And in 2006, I saw my dream… Male modeling *could* be the way. David James Gandy had just won a British competition like Tyra Banks' America's

Next Top Model. A gorgeous male model. If I had enough in the bank to put up as collateral, I would have sacrificed it all to bring him into JSS. I knew in my gut that he could sell ice to Eskimos.

Needless to say, I couldn't afford Mr. Gandy up against Select Model Management, but I took what I'd learned about his looks, and others who had been making it big, applied my Columbia education, and contracted twelve new faces to redefine JSS Models, Inc.

And it worked! *Thank you, Mr. Gandy and an Ivy League education.* In much less time than it took for William to break into the upper tier of model management, I found my way. I was hot. I was a trend-setter. I was respected. I was no longer Jackass Jack from Charter Oaks, Colorado. I had fully shed my old self.

Being a success was a thrill. I poured my whole self into my job. It was how I defined myself, for the most part. I guess I had always kind of thought I'd meet that right gal. We'd fall in love and get married. There was a time when I thought Kari was that girl. But as time went on, I saw that dream fade and I decided it was for the best.

I wasn't complaining. I was living most men's fantasy. Sleeping with women without commitment. Gorgeous women. I embraced my Dom side whenever I wanted, which was often. I came and went as I saw fit and it suited me. Many of my friends married and divorced. Some more than once. I saw their failed relationships destroy them, emotionally, financially or both. Becca and Rita were the exception. They were rock solid. They had their moments, but for the most part, they were the example of a fabulous relationship. On July 30, 2011, six days after the legalization of same-sex marriage in New York, Becca and Rita made it official. As for me, I settled into bachelorhood very nicely. But truthfully, after once or twice with a chick, I was bored. So, it was a footloose and fancy-free life for me. Simple and clean.

CHAPTER 18

April 2, 2013

Peter Allen was a godsend. An incredible manager. He thrived on the pace of the job, didn't mind the babysitting of the models with attitude and eating disorders that the job entailed, and reigning in the partiers. He'd just returned from a six-day on location shoot and was craving steak after being surrounded by the vegan and 'non-eating' models. So, we went to one of our favorite haunts, Ed Scott's Steak House, on Lexington. But as soon as we sat down, and Peter dove into the recap of the shoot, the photogs, and crew, and who said what, and did what, and with whom—I was entranced. Not with what Peter was saying. Fuck, I didn't hear any of it. I saw *her*.

I've been surrounded by 'beautiful people' my whole adult life. I'm surrounded by 'beautiful people' every day. But sometimes I see a 'beautiful person' that *radiates* beauty. Someone who has a beauty not just on the outside, one that's not over styled with makeup and hair styling and photo editing, but also a beauty on the inside. Much like Kari. The inner beauty isn't just kindness or demeanor, but a confidence complimented by a vulnerability. The 'girl next door' that glows. On the one hand, I was tempted to walk over to where she was sitting as she scrolled through her iPhone and ask her to be a model for JSS, but I couldn't seem to move.

I studied her. Her skin was an alabaster. Flawless. Clean, clear, and bright. No tanning. No wrinkles. I couldn't place her age. Her eyes were alluring. Her delicate cheekbones didn't need any makeup to enhance them. Classic jaw line. Her attitude said "I've been around, I know how it goes," but she seemed younger, as if she was trying to find her way, and excited about the possibilities that lay ahead.

When she smiled at her server, my heart swelled. That smile was genuine. Her smile reached every part of her body. Yes, I worked with models all day; models who would smile but you could tell it was an act.

As she ran her fingers along her neck, I wanted to run my tongue along the same path. I wondered if she'd spritzed with Chanel No. 5. Or did she even wear perfume? I wanted to know what she tasted like. When she caught me staring at her, I didn't look away. I held her gaze. I knew at that moment that I was a goner. She was mine. I was going to do what it took. I would sacrifice everything. Bachelorhood be damned.

She ate her salad quietly, while scrolling through her phone. Was she texting or emailing her lover? My blood boiled. I didn't want her to have someone else; I wanted her to be mine. Her tongue darted out to catch a drop of dressing left behind on her full lip, and I imagined that tongue doing all sorts of things. Those lips wrapped around my dick. That tongue licking slowly up and down my shaft. My cock twitched and throbbed in my slacks. He wanted to be buried balls deep in her.

As I continued to study her, I watched her grow a little unnerved. Why? Didn't she know how amazing she was? There was a little something about her that seemed familiar, but that was probably because I looked at women all day. It wasn't that she was a model, I was sure about that. I wanted to get up and walk over to her, but just as I was about to, her server went up to her table. The two chatted a bit, My Beauty paid her bill, and then nearly ran out of the restaurant, avoiding looking in my direction. I started out of my seat to go after her.

"She'll be back," Shelby called to me, as she set lunch down in front of where Peter and I were sitting. Shelby was the best bartender I knew; trustworthy and had a good heart.

"Who?" Peter asked.

"The pixie cut. She'll be back."

"What would make you say that?" I asked. Leave it to Shelby to not miss a beat.

"Just a hunch." She winked at me and I knew it was more than a hunch.

"You care to elaborate?"

"No," she said, suppressing a smile.

"So," Peter interrupted. "Any word on a new bartender to replace David?"

"Funny you should ask, we hired someone new today. *Her* first shift will be at lunch on Thursday." Shelby wagged her eyebrows at me and nearly burst out laughing.

She? Could it be the same she? My she? "Thursday? Really?" I smiled back. "I may have to stop in and welcome the new team member."

"That would be nice," she said. "Can I get you anything else?" she asked, glancing at our lunches.

"I think we're good. Thanks," Peter replied. I was already planning out my Thursday.

Returning to the office, Becca handed me the files for the agreements to be finalized for the upcoming shows and shoots for next week.

"All right. Out with it," she said following me to my office.

"Out with what?" I replied, smugly, taking my seat and pulling off my tie.

"That was no ordinary lunch. Lunch with Peter usually sends you back to the office ready to fire some poor girl. And I happen to know that the latest shoot gave Peter more than a couple of grey hairs and wrinkles. What happened at lunch?"

I regarded her carefully before I spoke my next words. I trusted her implicitly, but sometimes her cynicism got to me. "Do you believe in love at first sight?"

A laugh exploded from her. She knew me well. Too well. "Jack Stevens! Once-and-Done-Jack. A romantic!" When I didn't join in on her laughter, she grew quiet, leaned in, and studied my face like a doctor. "I never would have bought it. But looking at your face, and knowing you better than you know yourself, you've got it bad." She sat back and crossed her arms. "Okay, I'll bite. What's her name? Who does she work for? How did you meet her?"

"I don't know. I don't know. And I saw her eating at Ed Scott's."

She stared at me, stunned. "What do you mean, you 'don't know'? Didn't you talk to her? Since when does Jack Stevens not talk to women, especially a chick he wants to bag?"

I looked at her sternly. "I do not want to simply *bag* this *woman*. Becca. She. Is. It."

"So why didn't you talk to her?"

"I have no idea. I was enraptured? But I'll see her on Thursday."

Becca fell into a fit of giggles. "Enraptured. Oh, Jack. What are we going to do with you? And what's happening on Thursday?"

"Just a hunch."

CHAPTER 19

April 23, 2013
Three weeks later

I listened to her graceful steps softly descend the staircase. I heard her reach the foyer, her delicate heels, softly tapping on the marble. I strained my ear. The door wasn't opening.

Go to her! I shouted in my head. But I couldn't walk. I slowly dropped to my knees. I was defeated. I poured my heart out to her, and she still left. I showed her who I was. I begged and pleaded. I didn't even remember all of what I'd said, only that every word was true. I looked at the clock on my bedside. It was only four thirty-four. I'd planned on cooking dinner for her, but then she showed up early, too early. I hadn't even gone grocery shopping. She upended everything. She said that she was going back to Napa. I begged. I wasn't proud of it, but for Beth I'd do whatever it took. I pointed out why she should be with me, but my stubborn, strong girl had made up her mind.

I heard a couple steps in the foyer over the pounding in my head. I looked to the bedroom door. Was she walking back? Please let her be walking back. I can't move without her. I can't function. I looked at the clock again. *Four thirty-eight.* She's still here. She hasn't left. Why?

I started to get angry. Why wasn't she walking back? Does she want me to chase her? I'd just been chasing for the past weeks, and with more gusto this past hour. Kissing her. Telling her how much I treasured her and that I saw us together until the end of time, or something like that. But she walked out, and now she won't leave. Is this some sort of game? I was honest and not one word was a line.

She cried. My words meant something to her.

Four forty-one the clock displayed.

I had begged her not to go. I kissed her. She pushed me away. I told her that we were always going to be together. I told her I would wait. I'm waiting. She hasn't left yet. She's coming back! That's why the door hasn't—

The distinct clicking of the brass knob of the front door screamed from downstairs. I heard the roar of traffic on Third Avenue. "NO!" I cried out. Did she hear me? I tried to stand. Tried to get my legs to function. And then the door closed. The place was silent again. Had she walked through the door or was she still standing there? I saw it clearly in my mind. *She's leaning on the door, eyes looking up the stairwell to find me.*

I leapt to my feet and raced to the hallway and the balcony that overlooked the foyer. What I saw didn't compute. It was just the door. The floor. The artwork. Beth was nowhere. I stood there staring. It felt like only seconds or minutes passed until I could get my brain and legs to function. I ran down the stairs and flung open the door. I looked up and down Thirty-eighth. And up and down Third. And then I realized that it was dark. How did she disappear so fast? I checked my watch; it was already six-forty. When did it get to be so late? Why was time so out of control?

I staggered back into my home—no, my house. Without Beth, it was a house. I went to pour myself a glass of Scotch. The last time I was standing here, she told me she was leaving. I picked up the glass and hurled it against the wall, watching the crystal vessel explode and send shards of glass everywhere. I picked up the bottle of Macallan 18 and pulled a long swig from it as if it were simply a bottle of beer, willing the burn from the brown liquor to replace the burning in my heart.

I was lured to the oversized velvet chair like a siren. She loved this chair. She had been sitting in it only hours earlier. My eyes rested on the wine stains still on the carpet from the first night she was in my home.

*   *   *

"*When was the last time he made love to you and made you scream his name in ecstasy?*" I asked. *I'd caught her completely off guard with the question and I was immediately sorry, but then* she was on her knees in front of me. On. Her. Knees. *She had to stop or I was going to shove her against the wall and fuck her right now. But I didn't want to just fuck her. I wanted to own her.* Baseballs. Grandmothers. New York City subways, *I told myself to get my raging erection in check.*

I placed a foot on the towel she was using to blot the spray. "*Don't. It's an old carpet. I've been meaning to replace it anyway,*" *I offered, hoping to calm her down.*

"*It's a beautiful carpet, Jack. I'll clean it. I'll pay for it if I have to work doubles all month. I'm sorry,*" *she said, still attempting to clean the mess.*

Dom mode kicked in full boat. She was on her fucking knees! "*I. Said. Don't.*" *She stopped. My cock twitched at her clearly submissive tendency.* "*Look at me.*"

She raised her head enough to see me through her lush eyelashes. Oh fuck! *I was done for. I reached out and pulled her chin to fully look at me, the way a good sub would. I searched her face, and felt it. We were meant to be.*

*   *   *

I stuffed my face into the seat back to smell her shampoo. It was there, faint, but there. I gulped again at the Scotch, seeking healing. But it didn't help. I slid off of the chair and planted my face into the seat bottom, where her pussy had been, hot and wet—for me. I did that to her.

I replayed the unexpected afternoon in my head over and over, while sucking on the bottle of Scotch.

I woke to something cold and rough on my face. My eyes didn't open. I couldn't open them. My head ached. I smelled something rotten. I groaned and curled up on the cold hard floor. *Where in the hell am I?*

"Uh-huh, you keep groaning, pretty-boy. At least you're moving now," a muffled woman's voice bellowed. "I was getting ready to call an ambulance."

"Shhhh," I managed through the hangover-cotton that coated my mouth.

The cold continued to press all over my face. It was cold and wet.

And then it hit me. I opened my eyes and looked around. Becca was sitting next to me holding a cloth, but Beth? Where was Beth?

"Did she come back yet?" I choked out.

"Who? What the fuck happened here Jack? You didn't answer my calls or texts or emails for three days. I get back into town this evening and Shannon said you've not been in the office for three days. I come to your house and find you passed out in your own vomit wreaking of a whisky distillery. Several empty bottles of very expensive Scotch and others. You have a guardian angel with you, you know that?"

"Where's Beth?"

"I don't know. Why?"

My mind raced. "What time is it? You said how many days? What day is it?"

"Eleven-thirty. Friday night," she answered. She looked confused. I tried to get up, but the room spun around me and I started to heave, puking up air and bile.

Pain washed through me. Physical and emotional. "I need a shower and get to her apartment. She said she was going home. But she couldn't have. What we had was real. It was powerful. She couldn't just leave us. She has to still be here. I have to get to her apartment. Can you take me?" I pleaded. I felt tears burn at my eyes and stream down my face.

"Jack. Look at me," she ordered in the voice that I'd needed. I looked at her. "When did you last see Beth?"

"Tuesday," I answered, my heart pounding.

"Have you been drinking since Tuesday?"

I was shaking. My heart ached. I nodded, looking around me.

Becca took me into her arms. "Shhhh...." she soothed. "The only place I'm bringing you right now is the shower. And then you will eat."

"But—" I protested.

"But nothing. We'll figure this out when you're clean and fed." The look in her eye was full Domme mode, but not in the whips way. In the *I'm-your-best-friend* way.

By four o'clock in the morning, I was showered, fed and feeling mildly human. I watched Becca gather the bottles of booze, Scotch, vodka, rum… *Shit!* from all over the living room and kitchen. I stopped counting after she collected eight.

"You're lucky to be alive, Jack," she scolded.

"It just hurts so bad, Bec," I said, holding my head.

"Badly," she corrected. I *wanted* to laugh. Even when I was feeling my worst, she wouldn't let me be my worst. "Listen," she said, putting the last of bottles in the recycling bin. "Go to her. I can't believe *you*, of all people, let her walk out. Go to her, get on your knees, and beg, grovel, and-or seduce. Do what you have to. It's been as plain as day since that first day that she's your heart, Jack. Go get your heart back. Fight."

"She didn't choose me. My heart is broken. I don't think I can survive this. You know how it feels."

"Fuck you, Jack. Cut the pity party. You're Jack Fucking Stevens. Get some sleep and then go to her apartment. Get her back."

I got some shut eye, and Saturday morning, around eleven, I made my way to Beth's apartment building. Stepping into the lobby, Dominic, the building's doorman, greeted me in his surly manner. When I asked him to buzz Beth, he informed me that she had him call her a cab to the airport on Wednesday and he hadn't seen her since, and he didn't know when she was coming back. I asked if she had suitcases or anything. He wouldn't say. *Bastard.*

Fighting the hangover, I went to Ed Scott's to see if Tom or Shelby could shed any light on when Beth was coming back. Stepping into the bar, I nearly puked. Not from the smell of food, which didn't help, or the wall of alcohol, but from the emotional pain that had me riding a wave of nausea. Everywhere I looked I saw her. The table she ate at the first time I saw her. Behind the bar where she worked. My table. Choking down the vomit that threatened, and my pride, I walked up to Shelby who was chatting and smiling with some guy at the bar.

"Shelby, when is Beth working next?" I asked.

"I don't know, Jack. She called in Wednesday afternoon and quit. She's not returning my calls or texts."

"She's gone home," the guy said, his back still to me. Shelby looked at him, shocked.

"What?" I asked. He couldn't know what I was talking about.

"She's gone home," he repeated, and turned to me. *Fuck!* It was Kevin. The neighbor guy. The young, squeaky clean, gorgeous-enough-to-be-a-male-model-working-for-me guy. The other guy who my Beth was seeing while she was living in New York. I wanted to punch him in his camera perfect face. I flexed my hands to keep from balling them up and breaking his beautiful nose. But I'd been there and done that. I wasn't going there again. "And if you know what's good for Liz," he continued, "you'll leave her be." He did his best to stare me down, but I didn't flinch. Shelby looked at me sadly, and shrugged. *What the fuck?*

"The hell I will," I growled. I turned and marched out of there. I barely made it to an ally just down the street from Ed Scott's before I was dry heaving again.

She really left.

CHAPTER 20

"**B**uckle up, please, Mr. Stevens. We've been cleared for take off," Katie, the overly peppy flight attendant said, collecting my glass.

As I settled in for the six and half hour flight to Napa, I started to run through the past three weeks. How I'd met an incredible woman, who was a perfect match for me, who came into my life so unexpectedly, and obliterated everything I thought I knew. The plane started taxiing down the runway and the speed made me think about how quickly I had fallen in love with Beth.

When did I fall in love with her? I knew I wanted her when I saw her eating alone at Ed Scott's that fateful day. Was it that first night Beth was in my home? How incredibly adorable she was, on her knees. Or when I followed her down the hallway and pounced on her, and the way her body responded to my touch. Maybe. Was it when I realized I knew her? Or that first dinner out with her? Our quiet table at Bella Serra's and she let me order for her without a moment's hesitation, and full of trust. The easy banter over dinner.

Was it the first time we made love? Every time with Beth was making love. I was most surprised that many of my Dominant tendencies fell to the wayside. My history of simply fucking women, domineering over them, and bending them to my will disappeared. I wanted Beth to experience every pleasure; it was no longer about *my* pleasure.

But her submissiveness was so appealing, so natural... The night I first brought out the blindfold... She had given me many indications of her submissive tendencies all evening long, from the lobby of her apartment, to my selecting her meal for her, and the commands I'd given to her to undress in my living room.

I rested my head back and closed my eyes recalling that night.

*   *   *

"*Y*ou *are an incredible woman, Beth. I want you. I've never wanted to be with another woman the way I want to be with you.*" *I watched my words register with her. It was like she'd never heard them before. My heart ached for her.*

"*And how about you, Beth? Do you need me too?*" Please say you need me, *I pleaded silently. She nodded. I desperately wanted to hear the words, but I accepted the nod. The Dom in me sniggered. I was becoming a pussy for Beth. I was coming undone. I was feeling and sounding desperate.*

"*Stand up,*" *I said, reclaiming my Dom urges and made a mental note to not sound desperate again.*

She stood slowly, heeding my command. Oh fuck, yeah. She set her glass on the side table and faced me.

"*Take a step closer,*" *I instructed. And she did. My heart pounded for joy. "I want to see that lacy bra you wore for me tonight. Unbutton your blouse,*" *I continued, staring up at her.*

I watched her slowly unbutton her blouse and let it hang open. Unable to sit with my cock pounding in my pants, I stood and walked over to her, taking my place behind her. I pulled her back into me and pressed my hips into her so she could feel *what she did to me. Touching her neck, I shoved the silk blouse down her arms until it fell to the ground. I stepped back and took in her gorgeous back.* Oh how I'd love to take a flogger to her back and make it glow pink. *But there was more to uncover…*

I stripped her of her black wool pants, discovering that the back of her panties were all lace. Not satin, not a cheap thong—although, I'd love to see her ass in one—but a back of lace.

"*Fffuuck! So hot,*" *I hissed. Leaning in, my nose brushing along her thigh, I inhaled, taking in her musky scent. "Delectable." I felt her tremble. I loved that I could do that to her. If she only knew what she was doing to me.*

As much as I wanted to bend her over and fuck her fiercely, my hands itched to feel her body. I slowly explored all that was before me starting with her calves and backs of her thighs. I loved how she felt, toned under her skin, but she still looked soft and delicate. So many women in my industry were way too thin and muscular. Beth was a perfect mix.

Reaching her hips and waist, she pushed back against me. Aww, hell. *I needed to slow this down. If she kept that up, I was going to abandon the seduction and fuck her.*

I sat back in the seat about half a foot behind us, letting her stand for my viewing pleasure. Her silhouette was all woman with perfect curves.

I felt my throat grow thick with need. "Turn around," I whispered.

She obeyed my command, but only partly. She had her arms wrapped around her midsection. Her chest heaved with nervous breath. Of course she was nervous. I sounded like I was losing it, even to myself. I had to regain control. Give her back her confidence. Why she was lacking any was beyond my understanding. Women were tough to crack. I let her have her small protection, but not for long. I rather liked how her arms pressed her breasts together. I wanted to rub my cock between those globes, while thumbing those amazing nipples that were straining through the lace.

"Lower your arms. I want to see all of you." She listened. Perfect. In more ways than one. "Perfection," I whispered.

She rolled her eyes.

"You don't agree?" I asked.

"I'm far from perfection," she whispered, lowering her head.

"Trust me on this, Beth. Your body—is perfect."

I leaned in and ran my hand up the inside of her thigh and placed my lips below her navel. I prayed a silent prayer of gratitude. For this evening... for this woman... for this moment.

Revealing my deepest secret, I said, "Tell me you need to be with me."

"I do," she breathed.

"Say it," I growled. I pulled back and looked up at her, begging that she would see what she did to me. She made me feel insecure. In her humble perfection, she made me need to be needed. "Please. Tell me you need me."

Her eyes explored my face. "I need you," she whispered.

"Go upstairs. First door," I told her. She started but then looked back at me.

"Aren't you coming?" she asked, looking confused.

"I want to watch you walk. I want to watch you move." I need to calm my own flooding emotions! *I shouted in my head. I needed to get myself in check.*

Watching her body move was truly erotic. Okay, maybe this wasn't the smartest move. The lacy underwear. Those heels. But moreover — the way her body moved. Her first steps were tentative, but then her confidence grew. You could see her grow comfortable with her sexuality. Fuck! Reel it in, Stevens, or this will be over before it starts.

"Those shoes do amazing things for your legs," I heard myself say. She glanced back at me and saw that I was staring.

Our eyes locked and she started up the stairs. With each step she took, my cock twitched in my pants. She caught me as I adjusted my pants, and the smirk that hit her face was golden.

When she was halfway up the stairs, I made my way to the base of the staircase and started up after her. When she reached the door I told her to go inside, she paused. I swiftly ascended the stairs and stepped up behind her. She smelled so good. *I whispered in her ear, "Nothing to fear here. It's okay. I'll take care of you,"*

CHAPTER 21

"**M**r. Stevens, can I get you *anything*?" Katie, the ever-eager flight attendant asked with a sweet smile. "We've reached cruising altitude. Just six hours to go." Before Beth, I would have had Katie under me and over me, servicing me in every way imaginable. But now, all I could think about was Beth. Other women didn't do it for me anymore.

"Water, please." I said. I didn't want to numb the memories anymore. I was a man on a mission.

Sipping the cool water Katie brought me, I continued recalling the first time Elizabeth and I made love. Her gentle noises. Her body's responsiveness to my touch. Her breasts, how her nipples pebbled... for me. Her pussy, how wet it got... for me.

But she wasn't letting go and giving into the moment.

* * *

I slipped out of the bed and headed to my treasure trove of fun. Pressing on the wall, the secret panel popped open. All I needed was a blindfold to help Beth give into the feelings, and think less. By my eyes roved over all of the devices. The paddle. The whip. Handcuffs. All would be terrific fun. But I didn't want to scare her. I was sure that I could get her there, but not tonight. Tonight I needed to connect with her. I needed to claim her.

Glancing back, she was looking all over the room. Was she looking to leave? No! She couldn't leave. I had this. I quickly selected a long black satin multi-use piece of fabric. It could be used for binding a partner, but I planned to use it to blind.

I returned to the bed, her face turned up to me. I brushed my thumb over her sensual lower lip. "You think too much. We need to have you focus on your feelings. Not what you see."

Blindfolding a woman is incredible. I've always felt it's her ultimate submission. Some think restraints are, but no. When a woman willingly releases her ability to see what is coming—that is trust. That is submission. And it was a wonderful feeling.

After I secured the blindfold to her porcelain face, leaving those lips for me to focus on, I consumed them. Kissing tenderly at first, then more intensely. I sucked on her lower lip and chewed gently. Her moans were my reward. How I wanted my cock in her mouth. Was she skilled at fellatio?

I brushed my thumb over her lip and this time pressed it into her mouth. I commanded her to suck it. She didn't really seem comfortable. I commanded her to suck my thumb like it was my cock. Her willingness to push herself made me smile.

I remembered teasing her skin, her nipples. Watching her body tremble and grow more excited with each kiss and touch. Winding her up was a joy. She wasn't acting. Not giving me some show. She was genuine.

And Oh, fuck! she tasted incredible. I had given her her first orgasm of the night with my mouth clamped down on her clit and two fingers thrust into her soft, silky, and tight snatch.

"Yes!" she cried, her body quivering. But I didn't let her down. No. I kept it going, finger fucking her, so I could watch her body, and savor the taste of her on my tongue. And the way she dragged her nails down my back, nearly making me explode.

Then she started begging. It was a desirous plea. And she was asking for me. I pulled off the blindfold and caught her eyes. The surge that pulsed through me from that small contact was fuel for the fire that had been stoked into an incredible blaze.

I slowly pushed my raging, teenage hard cock into her as I stared into those huge, seductive, brown, doe eyes. Sinking into her hot, slippery, tight pussy took stages. The look on her face when I first slid into her was shock, then when I asked her if she was ready for "the rest" she almost looked horrified. But she didn't tell me to stop—my heart will always swell with the strength she exhibited.

After I had my full length sunk in, I was glad to be wearing a condom. It would have been over already had I not. I employed every ounce of restraint to not come once fully seated. And once she gave me the "okay" I tabled the gentleman in me and *fucked her hard. God, it was incredible. She was incredible. When I came, I practically forgot my name.*

But then she... She... Fuck! She brought his *name up!* Greg. *I would not let her disrespect us, what we were when we were together. The Dom in me kicked in. What can I say? It was a hard habit to break.*

I got out of the bed swiftly.

"W-What?" she stammered, clearly confused.

"Get up."

"Jack, what's going on?"

Of course I'd give her another chance. I already knew I would be nothing without her.

"How dare you bring another man's name into my bed? You need to learn a lesson, little girl."

"Oh, come on now. You're being childish."

"Get. Up. Now. I will not ask again, Elizabeth." Using her formal name let her know that I meant business. She dutifully stood before me, and I took her hand and lead her to the sofa, then bent her over my knee. With her glorious ass facing up at me, I almost lost my resolve.

She had started speaking, but I stopped her. This was about a lesson on respect. She had to recognize that our bed was only big enough for two. I slapped her bare bottom. I didn't use my full force, I didn't wish to bruise her, but I wanted her to know that I meant business.

"You need to learn to hold your tongue." I rubbed the place where I had slapped.

"I was just—"

My hand came down on the other cheek. I had to say my piece. I soothed that slap, and continued. "Speaking the name of another man in bed is extremely disrespectful." I delivered two more slaps without her objection. I nodded. She was getting it. Good Lord, this woman is perfect.

"When you are with me, you are with me. Do you understand?"

I waited. She didn't answer. I slapped again. I felt the shame and understanding radiate from her as much as the warmth of her rear under my hand.

"I asked a question. Do you need me to repeat it?"

"No, I understand. I'm sorry."

One more. I kneaded her glowing, pink bottom.

"Would you like me to talk about other women I have been with while you are cradled in my arms after mind blowing sex?" I said more gently. *I would never, because, well, for one I couldn't remember anyone else's name, in or out of bed.*

"N-No. I suppose I wouldn't."

"I didn't think so," I said, continuing my attention to her backside, relishing in delivering aftercare. *"So, are you done?"*

"Yes, sir." Fuck! She called me Sir. *I couldn't believe my fortune. Again, I admired how she was a natural submissive. I lowered my head and kissed her warm, tingling tush.*

"Good girl." I felt her smile. *I decided to test the waters with another, more playful tap.* Oh, hell! *She moaned! She was in subspace. She was a sub. With minimal training, she was a sub.*

"That one was for pleasure. Did you feel a difference?"

"Yes," she answered with a groan. *My cock leapt under her. Blood pounded in my ears.*

"So pink," I muttered letting my hand wander all over her perfect ass. *"So warm."* I chanced another playful slap. She shuddered. She fucking shuddered. She was aroused. Testing my hunch, I slipped my hand between her legs. She was dripping and the mew that escaped her throat as I explored her folds sent me over the edge.

I stood with her easily in my arms and plunked her over the arm of the sofa. Yanking open the drawer in the table just next to the sofa, I hastily slipped on a rubber then paused for just a moment for one question. "Are you ready for more? And will you remember who you are with?"

"Yes, sir," and with those two words, I fucked her so hard, my balls slapping against her, I almost feared a heart attack. Not just from the exertion, but from the overwhelming joy and love—yes, love—I felt for this woman. At the brink, I went for broke. I reached under her and took ahold of her breasts and rolled her nipples in my fingers, releasing her orgasm. Her pussy clamping around me, and her delicious nectar snaking out of her, I delivered two more powerful thrusts and let go.

*   *   *

Turbulence gripped the aircraft, jarring me from my most precious memory of Beth. I glanced over at the flight attendant who was biting her lip, her eyes unabashedly resting on my tented slacks. I reached to the collection of magazines and newspapers in the cubby to the left of the seat. Rifling through the wide variety with everything from this month's Vogue to today's Wall Street Journal, I selected the Journal and rested it on my lap, shielding Katie's view. She at least had the decency to look away after that.

CHAPTER 22

After finishing with the Wall Street Journal, and by finishing, I mean giving up on trying to read it, Katie served me lunch.

I loved private jet food. As good as first class food was, private was incredible. I thought back to my trip to Paris, the last time I'd been on a flight.

*   *   *

Beth had just been in my office trying to return the dress and shoes I'd given her for her birthday. It was never up for question. She was not allowed to return either gift. Getting a sneak peek at how she'd look when I saw her on the following Friday when I would take her to the opera was a bonus, a present of my own. I had been so riled up afterward, I nearly fucked her in my office. On the plane, I couldn't even eat.

And once in Paris, a city that had been privy to many, many trysts, Jean-Claude, my host, was eager to hit the town. Seeing that I was here for business, and I didn't want to offend JC by declining the private soiree he'd arranged, I went. I only half entertained the women who were there. After an hour, I had only talked with the statuesque models, however I wasn't much of a conversationalist. My mind was completely focused on my own model beauty waiting for me back in Manhattan.

JC noticed my irregular behavior as he returned from what was surely a coupling with one of the girls, his hair still mussed and his face flushed. "What is it, my friend? Argh zees beauteeful wemon not to your likingh deese days?" he asked with his thick accent, refreshing my Scotch.

"Mon amie," I replied cordially. "You could say my heart has been struck by Cupid's bow."

'Mon dieu!" he exclaimed. "Do tell. Whoo has captured zee heart of zee legendary Jacque Stevenz?"

"Beth," I replied, letting all emotion wash over my face. Even saying her name relaxed me. I was in love, and I didn't care.

The next day, after I'd wrapped up business, I hit the streets looking for something special to bring home for Beth. I visited a half a dozen shops before I found the piece on Place Vendome. Feeling like the King of the Mountain while strolling along some of the touristy places ending up in the Left Bank, I took a seat at the Le Coutume Café. As I sipped my espresso, I watched the couples and families walk and laugh. I considered how my life had made a complete turn-around in just two weeks. I had been a confirmed bachelor and happy with my life. I only needed my friends and I lived without regret. Now all I could think about was Beth, and not spending another day without her. I wished that I had kidnapped her Tuesday and brought her with me to Paris. She would really enjoy this. One day I'll bring her here. One day soon. We'll stroll together, we'll dine at bistros al fresco, and at incredible gourmet establishments. We'll…

Suddenly I heard a laugh from a table behind me that shot right up my spine. I turned and saw her. She was still beautiful, as if the past twenty years hadn't touched her. I stood from my table and dropped a few euro, lest the server think I skipped out on my check, and went to her table.

"Kari, fancy meeting you here," I said, putting on my best smile.

She stiffened and pulled her hand from the man she was sitting with. She looked petrified and I couldn't blame her. Not after what happened the last time I'd seen her. She was with that surfer-dude and I went all psycho on him.

"Jack, um, hi. What are you doing here?" Her eyes darted all around as if calculating my likelihood of pummeling a guy on this quiet pedestrian way.

"In town for business. You look wonderful, although I'm not surprised." I turned to the man she was sitting with, and stuck out my to shake hands with him. Kari jumped, but she needed to know I was no threat. "Bonjour. Jack Stevens. I'm an old friend of Kari's."

The man took my hand. "Bonjour. Phillipe Gauthier."

I took a seat at their table and fear and anxiety jumped onto Kari's angelic face. "Phillipe, mon cherie." She rattled off some smooth French, I think something about a croissant. Phillipe glanced at me nervously, but rose from the table and headed into the restaurant.

She turned to me, sitting up straighter, all business, no warmth. "What are you doing here?" she demanded. She had every right to be leery.

"Like I said, for business. Look, I'm no threat. I do want to tell you how sorry I am after…" I let my sentence drift. Admitting out loud that I had behaved so much like a caveman the last time was saw one another was not necessary. We both knew. "I was young. Well, not that young, let's just say I was stupid. Kari, we're good. Trust me. If you're with Phillipe, it's okay. So, who is Phillipe?"

"Just a friend," she said, her eyes darting into him standing at the counter inside.

"He seems like more than a friend. I'm surprised you're not settled and married with two point five kids driving a minivan. Are you living here? Or visiting? I remember how much you loved all things French."

She smiled and pushed her gorgeous long hair behind her ear. "I live here. For the past thirteen years, in fact. And actually… I have a son. Sébastien." A quick smile hit her face.

"And Sébastien's father?" I asked nodding my head at Phillipe, who was eyeing us from the counter.

She shook her head. "Matthieu is no longer with us," she said, her face falling.

"Kari, I'm so sorry," I whispered, my hand instinctively reaching to cover hers.

Phillipe returned to the table and slid a chocolate croissant in front of her. "Are we okay here?" he asked in perfect English with just a slight accent.

"Yes," she replied. She leaned over and placed a quick kiss on Phillipe's cheek. Her glance back to me was rewarded with a smile.

She relaxed and we spent the next forty-five minutes catching up. She graduated from Yale in 1997, and landed a job with a French-American firm. She quickly made a name for herself and in 2000, she relocated to Paris. Here, she met her husband, Matthieu, they married, and had Sébastien shortly after their second anniversary. Sadly, Matthieu was killed in a horrible car crash about six years ago, leaving her and her son Sébastien as a family of two. Sébastien had just turned ten. She met Phillipe in a single parents group last year. He was a widower of a little girl, Jeannette, just a couple years younger than Sébastien. I told Kari all about my company, and of course about Beth, and Kari seemed genuinely happy for me. I extended an invitation to whenever she found herself in New York. She said she would definitely call. I sincerely doubted it, but it was nice to at least have things on friendlier terms than our last interactions. I felt fabulous being able to apologize face-to-face. But nothing would compare to the face I saw in my dreams for the past two weeks, and for many years to come.

CHAPTER 23

I landed at Napa County Airport shortly after ten-thirty at night. I rented a car, a convertible, looking forward to a few sunny California days and prayed rain wasn't in the forecast. I knew the scenery was beautiful and was somewhat disappointed that I had to drive it in the dark, but the lack of such vistas allowed my mind to plan scenario after scenario of what I'd do when I saw Beth. It had been four agonizing days, more than half of which I'd spent sauced. Would she be outside? Would I have to knock on her door? What if *he* was home? Would I be able to keep from decking him like I had surfer boy years ago? I know he is her husband, but she had left him for a reason. And I know she thought she was doing the right thing by giving him a second chance, but he was not worthy of someone like her. He let her go. I wasn't going to let Beth go—ever. We were too perfect together.

I checked into the Hilton Sonoma shortly after eleven, eager for tomorrow—when I saw her. My Breath... My Beth. I should have been exhausted with the full day in New York and the six and a half hour flight, but my mind was not to be quieted. I took a hot shower, and chose to knock one off hoping that the expenditure would make me somewhat tired. I kept the knowledge that Beth was only a half an hour drive from me prominently in mind to get the job done. I thought about her eyes... her ears... her neck...her mouth. I fisted my dick roughly. I needed it rough. I needed to feel.

I recalled her standing before me blindfolded. I thought about her pink skin after I'd flogged her gorgeous back. I lost it when I remembered her ass pointed at me. She was so willing in all things. She trusted me. I imagined taking her ass with my cock. My grip tightened, quickened and I exploded with a roar.

Feeling somewhat relieved, and a little more ready for sleep, I finished my shower, dried off, and slipped into the crisp cotton sheets. I filled my thoughts with knowing that tomorrow I'd see her. Tomorrow would be my reward. Tomorrow, my heart would start to repair. There was no way she was going to say no to me. Just as I knew she trusted me, I had to trust that our connection was unbreakable.

I must have been more tired than I realized because I woke up at nine the next morning. It was already time for lunch back in New York. I got out of bed and was so tense, I decided to hit the hotel's gym after a light bite in the restaurant. It'd been days since I'd worked out. Everyone must have been out touring the local vineyards, because the gym was empty. That was fine by me. I put myself through a punishing routine. Two hours later, feeling invigorated, I headed back to my room, and showered for my reunion with my heart.

Opting for California casual, I dressed in khakis and a polo. I pulled up the email from Becca with Beth's address, and plugged it into the car's GPS. Around one in the afternoon, I pulled up to her house and parked across the street. The house was not as I imagined. Somehow I had pictured a farm style house, like the place in Colorado where I'd first seen her. But there wasn't a swing in the front yard tree. There was a large wrap around porch, but it was precisely arranged, not the warm collection of her childhood home. This was a house, not a home.

This house was new. And large. Current stylings. Nothing old world. A ranch. The only thing that said "Elizabeth" on this home, in my opinion, was the elegant wreath on the front door. Otherwise, it was cold. Yes, the home had a lovely view of vineyards, and I hoped there was a large deck off the back so Beth could sit and enjoy it, because the front was unbelievably prim and lacking in personality.

I turned off the ignition, climbed out of the car, and walked up to the front door. Taking a few cleansing breaths, and wiping my sweaty hands on my pants, I rang the doorbell, then knocked a few times for good measure. Waiting for her to open the door, I felt like a high school kid picking up his girlfriend for a first date.

I ran through my number one choice of opening lines that I was going to use, but then I started to go through the other opening lines I'd come up with on the drive. Which was the right approach? Declare that I love her and tell her I'm fighting for her? Or do I take the casual approach, that I happen to be in town for business? What if someone else answers, like her asshat husband? God, I hope not. I truly feared that if he answered, I might punch him in the face.

Peeking in the windows, I noted that everything was immaculate, but it also looked as if no one was home. I rang the bell again and checked the time. Had she looked out of the windows and seen me? Was she avoiding me? My heart ached at the possibility.

I pulled out my phone, and pressed speed dial.

"Yeah, boss. What can I do for ya?" Peter answered.

"I need a favor. Remember you were telling me about how you had to track Natasha a few weeks ago using her cellphone to find her and some GPS thing?"

"Yeah, sure. What do you need to know? I found her at the—"

"I don't need to know where you found *her,*" I interrupted. "I need to find someone else. How do I do that?"

Peter guided me step-by-step in finding and downloading the app I would need. Then I entered in Beth's cell phone number and let the app do its thing. I prayed that she had the GPS locator activated on her phone and when my phone vibrated and pinged indicating a successful find, my heart leapt for joy. She wasn't at home. She was somewhere downtown. I hopped in the rental and initiated the turn-by-turn of the mapping program to get me to where Beth's phone was.

Twenty-five minutes later, I turned into a parking lot of the *Napa Valley Women's Medical Center* and my blood ran cold. Why was she *here?* Was she okay? I fought every instinct in my body telling me to run to her and hold her. Sit with her and hold her hand while she went through whatever she was going through.

CHAPTER 24

The next hour and half was agony. I tried convincing myself that she was going for a routine visit that women had to do. Did she think she'd gotten some STD while with me and that Southern boy? Well, if she did, it was from him, not me. But Kevin didn't seem to be the kind of guy that was screwing chicks with STDs or carrying one himself. I might not like the guy, especially the fact that he was with Beth in the biblical way, but I had to be honest. Maybe it was one of those yeast things. I'd heard that too much sex could do that to a woman.

"Nine. But give me ten...please," I remembered her saying that day she'd come to my home and she begged me to make love to her, then she asked for punishment. Ten pops of the riding crop.

Sitting in my rented car, staring at the door, watching women enter and exit was torture. Every time someone came out, I had to look two or three times to make sure it wasn't her. A couple of times I'd walked up to the clinic's door, and one of those times I had my hand on the handle. I was going to barge in and demand to see Beth and know what was wrong. But I didn't want to embarrass her.

"Please God," I prayed. "Let Beth be fine." I sat, and confessed my sins from the past thirty some-odd years.

Finally the door opened and she came out. I didn't have to look more than once. I knew it was her at in an instant. My heart knew it. My cock knew it. She was as beautiful as ever, wearing a pair of faded jeans and a bright pink top. She held the door and a blonde woman, whom I assumed was Jessica from all that Beth had told me about her best friend from the third grade, came out and the two walked together to a black Lexus SUV. Beth looked fine. Tired, but fine. But her friend looked emotionally worn out. Maybe Beth was here for her friend? That had to be it. Beth was fine. Please. She had to be fine.

Beth opened the door for her friend to get in on the passenger side of the Lexus, but before Beth got into the drivers seat, she glanced at my car. She spotted me before I could duck into my seat. Maybe I wanted her to spot me. I wish I could have read her face. It was like twenty emotions hitting her at one time. Quickly, I got out and stood. Beth stood frozen. I extended my hand for her to take it. She eyed my hand, then searched my eyes. I knew what I was asking was wrong. She had chosen to come back to California. She was out with her friend for some medical reason. And I'd ambushed her.

Then, before I knew it, she was in front of me. My breathing quickened. I could smell her trademark rosemary shampoo and Chanel Mademoiselle perfume. I eyed her mouth. Her tender lips. I wanted to crush my mouth on hers. I wanted to nibble her lip. I wanted to run my hands on her gorgeous neck.

"Are you okay? Please tell me you are okay?" I asked, barely able to make the words.

She nodded and swallowed. "Nice convertible. What are you doing here?"

"I had business in San Francisco this past weekend," I lied. If she'd only known that I was drunk as shit three days earlier.

"You shouldn't be here," she said, her eyes darting all around as she surveyed the parking lot.

"I couldn't help it, Beth." Her eyes fluttered closed and she lowered her head.

"I love when you call me that," she whispered.

I crooked my finger under her chin and tilted her face back to mine. "You are still my breath. And my Beth. You always will be." I eyed the door of the medical center. "And you are telling the truth? You're okay?"

"Yes. I'm here with Jessica. She had some tests today, so I drove her," she said, her voice shaking slightly.

"Is she okay?"

"We'll know in a few days." She turned and glanced at her car. "Listen, we're headed to a late lunch. It was good seeing you. Have a safe flight back to New York."

"I'm not going back for a few days. Can I see you?"

"Jack," she sighed.

"I'd like to take you to dinner. There's a lovely place in Saint Helena. Tra Vigne."

"I know it," she giggled and bit her lip, the one I desperately want to suck into my mouth, and then started laughing.

"What is so funny?" I asked.

"It's on Charter Oak Avenue. An interesting coincidence." Yes, an interesting coincidence that the restaurant would be on the street with the same name as our hometown.

"Fate," I said, the desire in my voice evident, even to me. I hoped she heard it. "Tonight. I'll pick you up at six-thirty."

"You can't possibly—"

"Stay away from you. No I can't," I finished. "Please. I need to know that you're okay."

She didn't reply right away. She stared deeply into my eyes. I saw what I needed to see. We weren't over. I had a chance. No, I had more than a chance.

"And what am I supposed to tell Greg? That I'm going to dinner with you?" she asked.

"Tell him you're going out with an *old friend*," I offered. The choice of words was not lost on her. She remembered as well as I did our encounter in the lobby with Kevin.

"I'll think about it. I'll text you yes or no. But Jessica is in the car and—" she started.

"Of course. Go. Enjoy lunch. I'll see you tonight."

"You're awfully confident."

I just smiled. I was confident. Standing next to Beth, I was invincible.

I pulled out ingredients for dinner and poured myself a glass of chardonnay. I had been a lousy lunch date for Jessica. Today was about her. Today, Jess was getting a biopsy due to some abnormalities on her mammogram that her sister, Kimmy had taken her to last Friday. I don't know who was more terrified, Jess or me. Yet neither of us would let the other know it. We didn't have to, thirty-five years of friendship is good for that. Jack's unexpected appearance caught me more than a little off guard, but created a delightful distraction for Jessica. I finally spilled and filled her in on the finale of my New York adventure.

Since I'd returned late Wednesday from my jaunt to New York, Jessica had pumped me for information about all that went on. I kept tight lipped. I couldn't talk about it. Yes, she was my best friend, but because she was, she saw my struggle and let me have my space.

In short, after leaving Jack's place Tuesday night, six long days ago, I've cried no less than three times a day. I cried that whole Tuesday night, until I passed out at who knows what time. I cried in the cab ride to the airport. I cried half of the flight home. I seriously had no idea I could create so many tears. I started to chant "water my grass," as Kevin's *abuela* phrased it. *The grass is always greener where you water it.* I had to keep telling myself that over and over. I had to focus and figure out how I was going to water that damn grass named Greg. I thought my idea of surprising him would be fun, spontaneous, and sexy. But, he seemed rather put out and annoyed. *Keep trying. Don't give up. Twenty-four years is a long time.*

Last night's dinner I took a risk.

*   *   *

"*Soooo, you're quiet,*" *I said to Greg as he pushed bites of his Chicken Parmesan around his plate. Not that he was usually chatty at dinner,*

but I would think after a few days in a hotel with his wife, a wife who came back after being gone for three weeks, he might try harder.

I "understood" that Greg was quiet the first night. I'd surprised him and he said he'd not slept much the past couple of nights. I "understood" Friday when he said he was still processing my trip away and the "new" woman I had become. I had been gone for three weeks, and our "reunion" in New York was "different." I "understood" Saturday when we got home that he was "worn out" from the past few days, although he did comment that this was the second Saturday that he'd missed his round of golf with our neighbor Aaron.

"A lot on my mind, I guess. I was just looking over my inbox. Two new clients that I was supposed to meet last week, and now I have both of those meetings scheduled for tomorrow." He stuck a bite of chicken in his mouth and started chewing, but his eyes darted to his damn cell phone sitting on the sideboard. Since I got back, I've not allowed his cell phone to come to the dinner table. It was one of the things that kept us from communicating. Or at least I thought.

We dined just fine in New York when his cell wasn't sitting on the table with us. We talked, even laughed. I thought that maybe if the phone wasn't there, we'd be good. But then, when I thought about the rest of that night, talking about the fact that I'd been with Jack and Kevin while I was away, and that I'd been spanked and punished by Jack… And that I liked it. This past weekend, Greg said that when he spanked me back in New York, he didn't care for it and asked if we could never do that again. I felt my inner light dim, but agreed.

"I think we should see a marriage counselor," I whispered, then quickly took a sip of wine.

"Are you kidding?" he snickered. "We're fine. We're going to be fine," he said looking at me in earnest. "I'm sorry. I'll try harder. We don't need to air our dirty laundry to some quack."

"I think it might be helpful, that's all. Maybe they can give us some advice on how to reconnect. We've never been very good at that, Greg. I like conversation over dinner. Talk to me," I pleaded.

"Okay. You mentioned that you'd like to start looking at charities to work for. Where do you think you'll look?"

I'd already listed for him the four or five places that I was going to talk to, but, hey. It was a start—right?

*   *   *

I was trying to water the grass, only, it wasn't going as planned. And now, here was Jack. In California. Seeing him in the parking lot was a wake up call. Instantly, my heart started pounding. Not beating faster—*pounding*. I replayed the words he'd said in his living room when I told him I was coming back to Napa. *"Does he make your heart pound like this?" "Does he make you catch your breath with a mere touch?" "Does he make you quiver with need?"* and *"Do you get this wet for him? I don't think so. That's because we were meant to be, Beth."*

I'd replayed that night in his place as much as I'd replayed the earth shattering sex. What was I going to do? *I'm trying to water the grass.* Dinner last night, I made a small step in the right direction. I had to do the "right" thing. I had to keep trying.

I picked up my phone to text Jack his answer, that I couldn't accept his invitation, but Greg called, interrupting my text. Putting on my cheeriest voice I told Greg that I was just putting together dinner. Coq au vin. His favorite. Then he dumped on me that, as much as he loved our long weekend, having missed the couple of days last week he had to put in more time than he realized to be ready for some presentation on Wednesday. He wouldn't be home until late. I don't know why, but I shifted into Old Bets mode and said it was fine.

Then, shocking myself even more, I told him I'd call a friend or two and go out to dinner. Maybe it was spite, maybe it was that my 'lady days' started this morning, but I was crabby, and if Greg wasn't willing to work on us, why should I? I wondered what he would do if I told him that Jack was in town and has asked me to dinner and I was going to take him up on the invitation.

I hung up the phone and poured a gin and tonic with a fat lime squeeze and silently thanked Morgan tomorrow for restocking my office bar.

I knew it was a shitty thing to do—to cancel on dinner. But we had just spent four solid days together. And after last night's dinner, when Elizabeth suggested counseling? I couldn't imagine what I'd come home to tonight.

I've enjoyed the day at work—quietly. Everyone keeps to themselves here. I plowed through my two new clients and caught up on files that should have been dealt with while I was off *galavanting* with Bets at the Embassy Suites. And what a nightmare that was! I didn't think Elizabeth coming back would be awkward, but she didn't come back as my Bets.

From her showing up in bright pink underwear under a trench coat to her initiating sex whenever we were alone, and sometimes not so alone, she was a whole new person. In the back of the limo, which I successfully put off. I mean, the driver was in the front seat. What would he think? How trashy. Then at the hotel in the elevator. Doesn't she know that there are cameras in there? And what if the doors opened and someone saw us? She was sex crazed, which was great, but at four in the afternoon? In our room, sure, we had a go at it, but when I looked at her, the new hair, the wild sparkle in her eye... I didn't really know who she was.

I woke up early that Thursday morning and watched her sleep. Even in her sleep she was different. Now she chose to sleep in the buff. A part of me found that totally hot, but then as my eyes raked over her body, coming to a stop at her butt, all I could see were the markings that I'd seen the week earlier when I chased her down in New York.

*   *   *

"Holy shit! Elizabeth! What happened to you?" Elizabeth had just seductively dropped her pants, and when she turned there were red marks all over her ass. "Your rear. It has welts on it!"
When she blushed, I was even more confused. She should be alarmed!
"I asked Jack to do that," she said, her voice sounding odd.

I couldn't make sense of what she just said. She "asked Jack" to do what? "To beat you?" I asked.

"NO! It's not like that at all. This was punishment for all I had done since I was here. For being with Jack and Kevin. I asked for this," she said. Her eyes showed that she was dead serious.

"I don't understand. You're making no sense whatsoever." What was she talking about? Punishment? Then I heard the rest of what she had said. "You were with both of them?"

"Not at the same time. And it—the punishment—started with Jack a while back. He corrected me with a slap, and a caress, to teach me respect. He showed me he was in control. He didn't spank me and let me lick my wounds. He cared for me after. And it didn't leave a mark – that time. This time I asked for more."

"In control? He has to hit you to show he was in control?" My blood pounded in my ears. You don't hit a woman. EVER! Hell! You shouldn't hit anyone. Ever!

"It told me that he was going to take care of everything. And I could show him that I trusted him to not hurt me. It was – I'm saying this all wrong…" She sat in the chair at the desk. I watched her try and figure out what to say next. Someone better say something because I was speechless. "But, Greg," she continued. "Somewhere deep inside of me…it lit a fire."

"A fire? What are you saying? You liked it? You really liked it?" I didn't even try and disguise my distaste of what she just said.

"No," she shook shook head, small whisps of hair falling from their place. "I loved it."

Loved it? *Who in the hell is this woman?*

* * *

When I tried my hand, literally, to do what she asked—to spank her—as some sort of punishment or sexual play or whatever fucked up thing that guy had stuffed into her pretty little head, I felt sick to my stomach.

I prayed that she wouldn't ask me to try that again, but at the hotel she did. Killed the moment in an instant.

I wanted to be this man that she had in her mind, some aggressive Neanderthal, but I couldn't do it. In fact, the more I thought about her and those marks on her ass, and when I spanked her myself, and that she'd been with not one but two other guys in New York, I shut down. I told Elizabeth why I didn't want to have 'to do anything'—at least that day. She seemed a little hurt, but she understood.

I knew then that I would forever regret my giving her permission to sow her wild oats. I never imagined she'd actually do it.

She took her time away, tonight, I was taking mine.

CHAPTER 25

I decided to try and relax in the Napa sunshine with some reading at the hotel's pool while I waited for Beth's reply. She said she would *'text yes or no.'* When my phone vibrated on the table next to me indicating an incoming message, I quickly reached for the device. Spotting Beth's name on the screen, my heart started to race. *Please say 'yes,' I silently prayed.* I opened the text app.

> 5:49pm
> See you at 6:30p?

I nearly fell off of my chair.

"Fuck, yeah!" I shouted, garnering a nasty glance from the couple seated on the other side of the pool.

I quickly shot a text back:

> 5:49pm
> Wild horses couldn't keep
> me away. XO J

I dressed comfortably in Napa Valley chic—"broken-in" jeans from LUCKY, a bright, white linen button-down unbuttoned at the top and the sleeves rolled up, and loafers without socks. As I stood, knocking on her front door, I started second guessing my wardrobe. I didn't want to make her uncomfortable by being underdressed. I just wanted to be relaxed with her. Like we always were in Manhattan. She had looked so great in her jeans earlier, I hoped that I'd chosen wisely.

When she opened the door, I realized I'd hit a home run. She was wearing jeans, only, with the rest of her ensemble, I was dumb struck. I couldn't talk. Her shirt was the same color as the dress I had bought for her to go to the opera. The gorgeous salmon shade really did compliment her coloring perfectly.

My eyes followed every contour of her face and jaw. My gaze dropped to the pendant she wore. It was *the* pendant I'd gotten her in Paris. The chocolate diamond.

*　　*　　*

"I did a little shopping in Paris," I said, presenting her with the black velvet box that had been burning my pocket for the past two days. I flicked the small silver clasp and presented her with the pendant I'd found at the quiet jewelry shop on the Place Vendome after my meeting with JC and his team from Vogue. Her reaction was priceless. I watched her eyes rake over the princess cut chocolate diamond, and a few other white diamonds accenting the corners of the chocolate one. All resting in a swirl of white gold. The pendant reminded me of her eyes.

"Jack. This definitely crosses the line. I can't poss—"

"Beth. This is your necklace. Please, do not deny me." I stared at her, willing her to accept this gift.

"But Jack, this is too expensive."

"Don't spoil this for me. I've never had the desire to buy anything like this for anyone before. All of the women that I've ever dated have only wanted to be with me because I was a famous model, or the owner of a modeling agency," I pleaded. I didn't mention Kari; it wasn't necessary. "You were with me knowing full well who I was, and I don't mean the me of the past thirty years. You know my past. Where I come from. An uneducated family. I'm sure you know I'm the first to go to college."

She nodded.

"You want to be with me for everything that I am. Just like I want you for everything you are. You haven't judged me one bit. You have given your trust and your body to me. This is a small token as to how much that means to me."

Her eyes welled with tears as she looked into mine. I was not exaggerating when I said that I could look into those eyes for the rest of my days and be a happy man. I pulled a kerchief from my pocket and carefully pressed it under each eye, collecting the tears before they could stain her face or ruin her makeup. "No crying. You're too beautiful and your make-up is perfect. Don't ruin those eyes for me."

I was itching to see the pendant hang from her sensual neck and rest on her porcelain skin. Setting the kerchief aside, I worked the jewelry out of its hold. "May I?" I held the piece up for her. "There's a nice touch to this necklace that is perfect for this dress—a smaller pendant for the back, to take advantage of the dress's back, or lack thereof." I pointed out the smaller version of the main pendant that would grace her back. The thought gave me shivers.

She stood and turned, showing me the incredible back of the dress for which this necklace was made. "You have a gorgeous back," I breathed on her neck. Her scent mixed with her perfume was intoxicating. I fumbled with the clasp. Being this close to her, and when I'd had her back exposed to me, I trembled. I recalled flogging her to a glorious rose color. I was a mess. I wanted to grab her and sink my aching cock into her sweet spot. Finally finding success with the clasp after a few tries, I laid the back pendant down perfectly, then kept my finger trailing down her spine.

I leaned in and kissed the nape of her neck and pressed my arousal into her lower back, to which she responded by pressing her bum into me. Sitting next to her for the next five hours or so was going to be torture.

"Turn, I'd like to see the front," I groaned. But when she turned, I had a hard time looking to the pendant. Her eyes were full of desire. Slowly, I tore my eyes from hers and got a good look at the pendant resting just between the swell of her breast.

"Perfect. Just like you." I extended an elbow toward her. "Shall we?" I offered.

*   *   *

The pendant was now hanging from a shorter chain, but the longer chain would have hidden the gem in the shirt. I couldn't help myself. I reached forward and touched it. My eyes teared slightly. *Man, I was really turning into a fucking girl!* She vibrated under my touch. *There it is. Our connection.*

She smiled and brought her hand over mine that touched the pendant. "The rest of it is in my jewelry box. It just didn't work with this new blouse."

"New?" I asked.

"I saw it this afternoon when Jessica and I were shopping," she shrugged. "It just spoke to me."

"It certainly is your color," I agreed.

She locked the door, and I walked quietly with her to the car. After we were situated, I pulled out of the driveway. As soon as we took off down the road, I took her hand in mine. Touching her felt so natural. My fingers instantly found something that hadn't been there in most of our time together back in Manhattan. A solitaire and band on her ring finger of the left hand I held. Running my thumb over it, I glanced at Beth. She wouldn't look at me. "You look phenomenal," I said, avoiding the awkward elephant detected in the car.

Her right hand reached up and touched the ends that curled softly on the left side of her neck, just over that spot behind her ear, the spot that makes her moan when I kiss her there. I wanted to pull the car over and fuck her like a teenager. Everything about her made me crave her, when I was with her, and even when I wasn't.

"Thank you," she giggled softly. I loved that sound. I missed it so much. "My hair dresser still hasn't seen what I've done. He's going to pass out when I go in for my regular appointment. Neighbors and friends have really been thrown for a loop."

"Well, I think the style suits you perfectly." I had so many questions that I wanted to ask her. And so many of those answers I didn't want to hear. Had her homecoming been a happy one? A hard one? No matter how she answered those questions, I feared it would crush me.

"So, what business did you have out this way? Wouldn't business have been more in the L.A. area?"

Busted. "Well, location shoots can be anywhere. I thought perhaps a spread in the vineyards would be an interesting back drop." I hoped she didn't know that my job didn't entail location shooting for the models. I negotiated the models contracts, not where they worked. That was up to the client. She started to point out the vineyards along the way, the people (her friends) who ran them, and the varietals grown there. She said she could talk to any of them if the location worked for what I was thinking about. I should have 'fessed up, but I enjoyed her enthusiasm.

We turned off Main Street onto Charter Oak and into the parking lot of Tra Vigne. "You hungry?" I asked.

A smile exploded on her breathtaking face. "Starved!" she said.

CHAPTER 26

I jumped out of the driver's seat and ran around to open Beth's door, but she was already half out. "What are you doing?" I said, trying to sound as playful as I could. I wanted to open her door and hold her hand as I helped her out of the passenger seat.

"We're just friends, Jack. Remember, I live here. I *know* these people. They *know* me." She looked me in the eye conveying the rest of her message. I got it. She was a married woman here. My heart sank. But she did accept my dinner invitation.

I shoved my hands in my pants pockets, playing it cool, and winked at her. I could play by her rules. I didn't need my hands to win this fight. She'd be mine by the night's end.

Walking into the restaurant without touching her was agony. I wanted to have her slim hand in mine, or my arm draped around her graceful shoulders. As we approached the hostess stand, the woman behind the podium glanced up and smiled at us. I saw recognition in her face as she eyed Beth.

"Elizabeth Fairchild! It has been too long, and I love what you've done with your hair!" the pert brunette exclaimed with a slight accent. "Così chic!" she added in Italian as she rounded the podium to hug Beth and take a closer look at her hair. "But I didn't see your name on the reservations tonight, honey. Where is Greg? Parking the car?" she asked looking toward the door.

"No, Marissa," Beth answered, taking my arm and pulling me forward. I relished that she was touching me. Pulling me along. Calling the shots. It was quite a turn on. "I'm here with a friend of mine who is in from out of town. Marissa, this is Jack Stevens, an old friend of mine from New York." *There she is with that* 'old friend' *bit.* Of course, I did refresh her of the idea a couple of hours ago. "Jack, this is Marissa Mancini. Marissa was one of my first friends in Napa Valley."

It would figure I'd choose a restaurant where Beth would know people.

"Oh," Marissa cooed, looking me up and down. I wasn't unaccustomed to such attention and generally I liked it, but not anymore, and especially since I was standing next to Beth. "Yes. Stevens. I did see that name on the list. And I have your table as requested." She shot a look at Beth, cocked a perfectly shaped eyebrow at her. I was suddenly very nervous that I had made things uncomfortable for Beth.

We were led through the restaurant to the patio and a very secluded table for two. We passed under the arched trellis that served as doorway to the table I had requested, and got a very interesting look from Marissa. I couldn't see Beth's face, but I could see that her neck had flushed a delicious crimson color. I suddenly wished I hadn't been so bold in my table request, but in the same wish, I just wanted to be alone with Beth.

Once we were seated, I noted Beth's unease. I took her menu and set it with mine. "I'm sorry. I shouldn't have been so bold."

"No, it's okay," she said turning her gorgeous brown eyes to me. "I've always wanted to sit at this table. I just have to make sure to chat with Marissa later. It's good, really."

"How is Jessica?" I asked, changing the topic, taking her hand in mine.

Beth sighed. "She's okay. Handling all of this so much better than I would. So, a couple weeks ago she found a lump, and—" She took a steadying breath. I held her hand a bit tighter. "You don't want to hear this..." she said her voice trailing off.

"I do. If it's important to you, I want to hear all about it." She looked at me, disbelieving. "Go on. What did her doctor say?"

"She went with her sister late last week for a mammogram and the doctor found a couple of abnormalities. This morning, I took her in for a biopsy. I would be out of my mind."

I lifted the hand I'd been holding and kissed the back of it. "I would be at your side every step of the way. When do her results come back?"

"Could be as early as tomorrow, but doubtful. Probably Wednesday or Thursday."

"If there's anything I can do, please let me help."

"You are something else."

"If it's important to you, it's important to me." I searched her eyes. They were full of sadness and concern. "I'm sorry you came home to such heartache. I'll put in a call to the medical center and have them move Jessica's tests to the top of the pile. She'll have her answer by tomorrow.

"You don't have to do that."

"I want to. Jessica needs peace of mind. Doctors play God with taking their time, not realizing the impact their actions take. Like a round of golf is more important. It's done and you can't stop me."

"Jack Stevens, you amaze me." The way she looked at me made me feel like the king of the world. I vowed right then and there that I would do anything and everything to keep that smile there. "Okay, where is that waiter?" she asked. "What? I told you. I'm starving! I could eat a horse!" she said, perhaps noting my expression. Just like the first time we went out for dinner, I loved the refreshing change of pace to eat with someone who actually *ate*.

As if on cue, a waiter appeared. "Marcus! So good to see you! How was your first year at Napa Valley College?" she asked him. *God, did I ever choose the wrong place to dine quietly.*

"Really good, Mrs. Fairchild. Your advice on the courses schedule was perfect, thank you."

"It's the least I could do. Would you be a dear, and bring us a bottle of the …"

I had not yet looked at the menu, but Beth took no notice. Or didn't care. I had no idea what just happened, but Beth took the reigns full on and ordered us an entire meal. From Primi to Secondi to Dolci and the wines to go with each. I was somewhere in limbo between feeling completely emasculated to totally impressed and turned on. Wasn't it my job to order for the lady?

"I'll be back in just a moment," Marcus said and slipped away.

"Well, I am impressed," I said, opting for the high road, and took a sip of water.

"You could say I *know the menu*," she said, smirking. God almighty how I wanted to consume that mouth of hers. But no chance as the sommelier appeared quietly presenting a bottle of wine to Beth.

"Thank you, André, but Mr. Stevens should have the honor," Beth said, shooting me a glance. *This woman will be the end of me*, I thought. And I'd like it no other way.

CHAPTER 27

We started in with our Sangiovese, and, as the first course of Beef Filet Mignon Carapaccio arrived, she grilled me about business, and what JSS was doing in California. I fed her a complete line of bullshit and felt horrible about it, but I didn't want to rock the boat by telling her I was here for her and her alone.

"I'd really love to get *you* in front of the camera," I said. "Maybe that's why I came."

"You're funny, Mr. Stevens. I'd never realized how comical you could be," she replied. As she sipped her wine, I realized that she really, truly didn't see what I saw, and likely what everyone, men and women alike, saw when they looked at her. A gorgeous woman with girl next door appeal. Beautiful, yet approachable.

"You really have no idea how stunning you are, do you?" I asked. I reached up and brushed the back of my fingers along her jaw and down her neck. I watched her eyes flutter closed as she tipped her head to the side so I could easily enjoy the graceful lines of her neck that left me in the most uncomfortable way. Where I initially thought my comfortable jeans would afford me space, should the beast in my pants misbehave, I was sorely mistaken when it came to the flood of emotions and feelings I was faced with when it came to Beth. What I wouldn't give to be having this meal back in my room at the Hilton Sonoma. Dinner would be done and I'd have her stripped bare, taking every inch of my dick in her perfect pussy. She'd be looking at me with those fuck-tabulous eyes. I'd have her begging me to let her come.

Interrupted yet again, the second course arrived. Beth had ordered a venison loin with cabernet sauce for me, and a fish dish with artichokes and capers for herself. Glasses of wine, hand selected by the sommelier, were brought to accompany each dish.

I asked what her plans were now that she'd come back to California. Silently, I prayed that she wasn't sure she was going to stay, or that she'd made a mistake and would say that she was packing her things and coming back to New York with me. I wanted to tell her that I'd already made flight arrangements for her to come home with me on Saturday, but as she talked about the opportunities she was looking into here in Napa, I felt about two inches tall.

"I really think I'd be good at the charity fundraising. I've done my fair share with the kids and their schools. It would be nice to work for a larger organization. With a far reaching purpose, you know? I'm going to look into the hospitals and local organizations this coming week."

"I think you would be marvelous at whatever you put your efforts to. You know, JSS has many charitable functions throughout the year. You could work for me." She looked at me, eyes-wide and stopped chewing. "On the West coast here, of course," I added.

She nodded nervously, and finished her bite.

"I'm sorry to have overstepped," I apologized.

"You have nothing to apologize for, Jack. I'm just—" she took a sip of wine. I watched her think. What I wouldn't give to know what was going through her mind.

"How's Phoebe?" I asked, swiftly changing topics. Helping Beth's daughter get the interview for a network internship, and greasing the wheels for her transfer to NYU cost me a few favors, but if it made Beth happy, it was worth it. Beth relaxed and launched into telling me about the internship Phoebe landed at the network where I'd set up her interview.

"You didn't have a hand in her getting that internship, did you?"

"She got the internship?" I hadn't heard that she'd gotten the spot. I was so proud of her. She really was a terrific gal. I only hoped that the studio didn't chew her up and spit her out. "I swear, I only got her the interview."

This is what a dinner should be like. Pleasant chatting. Humorous banter.

Since I've gotten home, dinners with Greg have been awkward. I wasn't sure if it was that way because of my "stunt" as he'd called it, or if that's how Greg and I just *are*. Before my trip to New York, he was texting or working on a file during dinner, or wolfing his dinner down so he could get back to work. Since I've returned, he just sits there and makes small talk like we're strangers. The kids, our day, the weather. I know I've only been back for five days, and half of those days were at a hotel, but even at the hotel...

"Can I tell you something?" Jack asked, interrupting my thoughts.

"Anything," I replied, sipping the wine.

"I've been in love with you since the day I saw you at Ed Scott's eating your salad."

"Jack, I—"

"Let me finish," he said, quieting me immediately. "Most of my life I've dominated women. When I told you that I was a Dominant, it was only part true. I'm actually a 'switch.' Sometimes I'm the Dom, sometimes I'm the submissive. But you are the first woman who has dominated my *heart*. You are the first woman that let those urges subside. I love being with you, and listening to you, and being happy for the things that make you happy. But most of all, I love being with you for how you make me feel about me. I've told you before that I'm a selfish man. I want you. Nothing more."

I swallowed and let all of that roll over me. The Dom/submissive bit, the love... the happiness. If this were a movie, I had no doubt that he'd be producing an engagement ring.

Dinner was then set before us, thankfully breaking the tension a bit. When Marcus left, I looked at Jack. I didn't know what to say.

"We don't have to talk about this. Let it sink in, Beth. But I mean every word of it." He searched my eyes. "Now eat. That's the Dom in me speaking." He winked, making me laugh a bit, and blasted me with a huge smile, a smile that radiated from his whole body. Like a huge weight had been lifted off of his shoulders, even if that burden was now, in part, dumped on mine.

"Now, tell me about Phoebe's internship," he said, and like that, he moved the conversation into shallower waters.

CHAPTER 28

The rest of our dinner was easy going as Beth spoke about Phoebe's upcoming internship and that Phoebe was going to stay in her old apartment, while Kevin agreed to keep an eye out for her. She asked me if I would, too, which of course I promised I would, and I meant it. Then she dove into talking about Bradley and Carter. Before long, we were sipping espresso and a chill had settled in the valley.

As we drove home, Beth continued talking about the charity work she was looking into in the area. Suddenly, I couldn't take it. The nearly full moon sent an impossible glow on her features and I needed to kiss her.

Quickly, I pulled the car over and threw it in park. I leaned over and kissed her. She tensed momentarily, then moaned and leaned in. Her soft pink tongue licked at the seam of my lips and my cock, already semi-hard all night long from sitting across from her at a hopelessly romantic table for two, was now as hard as steel. My fingers sought the delicate curves of her jawline and neck. I felt a calm rush through me, immediately followed by a consuming need for more. I wanted more, so much more, but not in a rented convertible. Then she sucked in my bottom lip in her super cute and seductive way. Our lips separated and our tongues slipped together. So comfortable and perfect.

Her arms came up and around my back, her nails raking at my shoulders, driving our passion further. I slid my hand down her front until I found her gorgeous breast, my hand forming around it. I could feel the delicate lace through the salmon silk that separated my hand from its prize. Her nipple was already pebbled.

I wanted her so badly, but not in a rented convertible. "I'm at the Hilton Sonoma. Come with me," I urged, my lips not leaving hers.

I felt her hands at my chest, but they weren't reaching for the buttons of my shirt. No, she was pushing back. Reluctantly, I let her. *Shit.* I saw it before she said it. I went too fast. I'd overstepped.

"Jack, this was a mistake. I came back to Napa to do the right thing. I'm trying to water the grass."

"Beth, what we have is no mistake. I know you feel it. Right now you're listening to your head. But what does your heart say?" I searched her eyes. I could see her heart. She was never very good at disguising her feelings from me.

"Please, take me home." She fell silent and melancholy. My heart ached for her. Her struggle was clear on her face, even if it was as plain as day in her heart.

I drove those last five minutes to her house, with only radio breaking the silence. Part of me was at peace. I had Beth back at my side. But a piece of me was still ripped up inside. She'd pushed me away. I wanted to ask her if she was happy that she'd come home. I wanted to ask her if her husband was treating her right. However, I only wanted to ask those questions if the answers were 'No' to both questions, and then I'd drive us straight to the airport and we'd fly back to where she belonged—in New York, with me.

In her driveway, I turned the car off.

"Dinner was lovely. It was good seeing you again," she said, not looking at me. She reached for the handle.

I hit the button for the lock, stopping her from leaving. "Why did you say yes?" I asked. "Why did you agree to have dinner with me?"

It wasn't like Beth to be a tease. She ruled with her heart. She'd said *yes* because she wanted to be with me. That's where her heart was safe, and she knew it. I picked up her hand and rubbed my thumb over the back of her knuckles.

"I'm sorry, Jack. I'm trying to do the right thing. Twenty years—I can't explain it to someone who's never been married. I came home to water the grass, but—And then I saw you this afternoon. And I was going to text you and say no—And then he called and needed to work late..." She blabbered, her voice quaking. She bit her lip to stop herself from going on. She was struggling. I hated to see her like this. I sat quietly, letting her talk.

"What, Jack? What are you thinking?" she asked.

She was so strong. I envied her. I was a mess, yet she was strong.

"Are you happy?" I asked.

She didn't answer, her eyes fixed out the window. I searched her profile for the answer, and I could see it. Her jaw slightly tensing. Or maybe I was convincing myself of what I wanted to see.

"Is Greg taking care of you?"

Her lip started to quiver. My heart broke. She wasn't happy. That ass wasn't treating her right. I pulled her into my arms, kissing the side of her head, when I really wanted those lips again. But now wasn't the time.

"It will take time," she whispered. "I'm sorry."

"You can't force your heart, Beth. What does your heart say? Because mine is saying that you complete me. Without you, I'm half a man."

A tear leapt from her eye and flowed down her cheek. I started to well up as well. *Think, Jack! Think! Fight!*

"I have to go see a few more locations tomorrow—for business. Would you like to come? You mentioned you knew the vintners near the restaurant. You could help me get in and scout the place."

She turned to look at me wide eyed. "Which vineyard?"

"I think you said the names were Don and Rebecca??"

"Dan and Rachel?"

"That's it! Yeah. Do you think they would be open to a shoot?"

"I can call her in the morning. You probably won't be able to get in until after the lunch hour."

"Perfect. Call me when you have our appointment."

She laughed softly. "Is this what it's like to work for you?"

Her laugh. That's so much better than her tears. I reached up and dried her cheek with my thumb. "Are you applying?" She laughed again and shook her head again. "Stay put," I commanded.

I unlocked the doors and got out, racing around to open her door for her. I helped her out and gave her one last look. I searched for a cue from her that I could kiss her, but her eyes flicked to the front of the house, and I decided against it, in case *he* was looking out the window at us.

"Call me tomorrow?"

She smiled and nodded. With a gentle squeeze of my hand, she then let go and walked to her front door. I waited until she was inside and a couple lights were turned on.

Unwilling to stand around and see if *he* was inside and came to her, I returned to my car and pulled out of the drive.

The moment I stepped inside, and flicked on the lights, I missed Jack's presence. He made me so comfortable, even with the hard stuff. Telling him that I was home to water the stupid grass. Was Jack right? Was my heart the one I should listen to? Or was it my head? Truth was that my heart *did* feel complete with Jack.

I looked at the entry table. Greg's keys weren't there, where he'd always left them. I looked at my watch. It was a quarter after ten. Was he still at the office? I looked around the house, ending up in the bedroom, thinking maybe he'd come home so tired and just brought his keys to the room and left them on his dresser.

Nope. Greg wasn't home.

This was wrong. It was *all* wrong. That I had left three weeks ago was wrong. That I had come home last week was wrong. How had I started down this slippery slope of stupid choices?

With a heavy heart and not knowing what to do, I slipped into my pajamas and into bed. What was supposed to be a second honeymoon was definitely over. *Shit.* Who was I kidding? It never began.

It had been an emotionally exhausting day. Jessica's doctor's appointment. Seeing Jack. Greg canceling dinner. Going out to dinner with Jack. I let the exhaustion of the busy day wash over me and put me to sleep, with a small joy in my heart. Tomorrow I would see Jack again.

Slipping into the house quietly, well after midnight, I checked the bedroom. Elizabeth was tucked into bed and sleeping quietly. *Thank goodness.* I wasn't in the mood for her throwing herself at me like a common slut. The wounds were still too fresh, especially when my liver was soaked.

Whenever she came home from dinners with her girlfriends, she was usually tipsy. And when her new personality, little-miss-I-like-sex, was tipsy, she was aggressive in bed. I should have liked it, but I didn't. I didn't like her in control. But the control she wanted me to take, I wasn't willing to exercise. And all this came from either Jack or Kevin...

What a bitch!

CHAPTER 29

Idrove back to the Hilton Sonoma filled with hope. I'd get another day with Beth. But what in the heck was the "watering the grass" shit she was talking about? I felt it was pretty obvious that things hadn't gone as planned with Beth coming back, and that her ass of a husband wasn't "trying" as Beth had said back in New York. She was home less than a week and he was letting her go out, not aiming to spend every minute with her? For her to give him that leeway that "it will take time." Did she really feel that way? Did she really think so little of herself?

I knew I was an ass for pursuing her, but I couldn't help myself. She was my breath. But she wasn't even home a week and he was already bailing on dinner? I felt somewhat guilty for fighting for a married woman, but so much of Beth screamed 'not-married.' And there was so much comfort in the two of us. Conversation flowed, we laughed easily, there was no apology when we were together.

Tomorrow, lunch with Beth in a vineyard. I fired up my laptop and looked for places to supply a picnic lunch. Brittany's Baskets Catering had great reviews and terrific looking menus, so I ordered a nice French themed basket of cheeses, fresh fruits and bread, with a bottle of Napa Chardonnay. I hoped that a pick up time of eleven would work.

I could see the whole thing play out in my head. We'd look over her friend's vineyard for the photo shoot—that wasn't on the books—I'd deem it perfect, and then I'd pull out the picnic basket, spread a blanket and it would be impossibly romantic. I couldn't wait.

The next morning, I was up before the sun. But for my internal clock, which was still on East Coast time, it was already seven in the morning and I was usually working out at this hour. Not one to break with certain routines, I hit the gym, even though it was four a.m. After all, keeping this body in top shape at my age required just as much work as it did when I was twenty.

Following my workout, I made a couple of business calls to New York, checking in with Becca and Peter. Things were going as scheduled—or *re*scheduled, as it was, and I could rest easy. Around nine, I put in a call to the Napa Valley Women's Medical Center for Jessica's results to be addressed sooner than later, and made a more-than-generous donation to the facility.

Finally, Beth called around ten and said that Mark and Ana had the more incredible vineyard, that we could visit at noon, and that she'd meet me there. As much as it irked me to let her drive herself to the vineyard, I knew that if I was going to win her back, it was going to be on her terms. So, I agreed to let her drive herself. Besides, it allowed me more time to find this Brittany's Baskets place and pick up our lunch. She gave me the address for my GPS and made a quick goodbye.

Not wanting to seem over eager, I took my time and got to the vineyard shortly after twelve. I pulled up into the parking lot and nearly crashed the rental when I got a glimpse of Beth. She was chatting with another couple, but looked up when she heard my car and the smile that burst across her face seized me. She wore a long, white, flowey, hippie skirt with a silk, turquoise tank top. As perfect as the salmon color was on her skin with her hair, the turquoise was equally stunning. I couldn't help but wonder what kind of panties she was wearing, or if she was wearing any at all.

I got out of the car and fought the urge to run to her, pull her into my arms, and kiss her deeply. Something about this whole region was making me a soft romantic, but I didn't care. I locked the car and strode up to Beth and her friends.

"Jack. I was starting to worry that you'd gotten lost," she smiled. "I'd like you to meet Mark and Ana Lawson. They've owned this vineyard for twenty-three years already. Wait until you see the gazebos they have at the back of the field by the lake." I shook hands with Mark and Ana and instantly liked them.

We toured a few places on the ranch that would make for nice back-drops for a photo shoot. When Ana pressed me for details about the photo shoot, I made up a story about wanting to feature some of the new faces our agency had brought on. I took notes in my iPhone, including my bullshit story, so I could send them to the PR department and pray that they could set something up.

Around one-thirty, I thanked the gracious couple, and asked if *Elizabeth* and I could use one of their gazebos by the lake for a light lunch. They said it would be perfectly fine and we parted company.

"Lunch?" Beth asked, turning to me after she hugged and kissed our hosts.

I shrugged. "I picked up a little picnic. I hope I wasn't too presumptive."

She looked at her watch. "I guess I have time. What did you bring?"

I ran back to the car, pulled out the perfectly packed lunch, and returned. She was surprised with the basket and we made our way to the quiet gazebo tucked back off the lake. I unpacked the spread on the floor of the gazebo and watched Beth as she took it all in.

"I've said it before, but you're amazing," she said.

"*You* are inspiring," I replied. I reached out and took her ankle, the one that had the temporary tattoo Kevin had given her for her birthday. I rubbed my thumb over where the offending—albeit temporary—ink sat. Then again, I should have her branded as my own. I could just imagine the name *Jack Stevens* penned permanently around her delicate joint. The thought made me chuckle. I extended my hand and helped her down to the blanket.

I was opening the wine, which had stayed nicely chilled in a space aged bag when Beth's phone rang. The ring tone made me laugh. Where she'd assigned her sister an old time car horn, this ring tone was Cindy Lauper's eighties hit *Girls Just Wanna Have Fun*.

"Oh! That's Jess, hang on a sec," she said digging into her purse. She saw me raise a brow at her, "What?" she asked me, giggling. "Hey, babe." she said answering the call. "Yeah, sure, what's up?... Uh-huh... Right...Omigosh! You're kidding! No, of course you're not kidding! Jess, that's awesome!... I love you... I will... Backatcha."

"Well, that sounded like a good call?" I asked, pouring the wine.

"The goodest!" she squealed. "Sorry, the best! Jess just heard from the labs. Her samples are benign. I can't believe that we didn't have to wait until tomorrow for the results. They always tell you one or two or three days, and it's always three days or four."

A smile burst on my face. "That's terrific."

She eyed me carefully. "What are you not telling me?"

"I know that waiting for critical news is a bitch. I called the clinic and had them move her samples to the top of the pile. I told you I would."

"Thank you," she said, taking the glass I offered her.

I clinked the glass she held. "To *friends*," I whispered.

"And wherever that road leads us," she finished the toast I had offered that first night she was in my living room, before she sprayed my carpet with the wine. I smiled, hopeful that all was not lost. If she remembered that small toast, she likely remembered so much more.

CHAPTER 30

Lunch continued, laughing and chatting, in the comfortable way that Beth and I had. The combination of the setting and the way she touched her neck, and the twinkle in her eye, I desperately wanted to lay her back and make sweet love to her.

"This is nice," she said, popping the last wedge of peach into her mouth, past those incredible lips, with a drop of the juice resting on them.

I wanted to lunge at her and slurp up that drop. The one question in my mind that I wanted to ask but I didn't want the answer to, slipped out of my lips instead.

"Has your homecoming been what you were looking for?"

She drained her glass of wine. That couldn't be a good sign. "Not exactly," she whispered.

With those two words, my heart was torn. On the one hand, she wasn't being treasured the way she deserved. And on the other—the hand I preferred—the door was open more than a crack for me.

"Come back to New York with me. I'll make sure you have the homecoming you deserve." The fact that she didn't blurt out 'No!' was definitely encouraging. I reached forward and dragged my finger across her lower lip collecting any of the juice I could find, and dipping my finger into her mouth.

Her breath quickened and she suckled my finger expertly. My cock ached but I bit my lip until it nearly bled, to cap my urge to sink myself balls deep into her. The door was a little more open than I thought.

"Jack, you're very naughty."

"I could be naughtier," I suggested raising a brow.

"Oh, I know you can," she said with a steady gaze. "I never did thank you for my punishment," she breathed.

"I'm sorry," I said. "I was too—"

"You were just what I needed. I asked for it. I liked it."

My mind was flooded with my activities after Beth had come to me, begged me to make love to her, and then asked for the paddle and crop.

*   *   *

The brisk walk to the apartment on East Fifty-first Streed did nothing to soothe my mind. The misting rain didn't touch the heat that threatened to consume me. How could I have done that to her? My Beth? My Breath?

I was still in a twisted mess when I unlocked the door and stepped into my 'home away from home'. The scent of wood and leather instantly hit me, the first calming I'd felt since that final POP.

I shucked my jacket, hanging it on the hooks along the wall by the door, then walked to the center of the room and dropped to my knees on the dark hardwood floors. And waited.

The last of the sun started to fade, leaving the room dark, enveloping me. Hugging me. Matching the inside of me. Where was B? Why was she so late? I needed this now. I closed my eyes and tried to process the past hour.

My mind continued to race, my breath matching my mind. She had come to me. She trusted me. She wasn't into the lifestyle. And to let her subject herself like that. Her choices were good ones. But she'd only had my hand until then. The paddle would have been enough.

"Jack, honey are you okay?" Her voice interrupted my thoughts, bringing relief. My punishment was almost delivered. But why was she breaking protocol? Why was she talking to me like a friend?

I opened my eyes. The room was now bathed in the warm glow of the low voltage lighting. I found Becca's eyes and begged her silently to get on with it.

"Oh, I see," she responded, straightening her six foot stature. "Choose your device and return to me."

Ah, I sighed. Commands. I could work with those. "Yes, Mistress."

I stood and walked to the closet. I returned only seconds later with the nine-foot longtail in hand. She took the whip confidently, issuing a curt nod, and stood poised in the center of the room.

"Shackles or horse?" she demanded.

I swallowed hard. "Shackles, Mistress."

One curt nod, and I raised my arms out to my sides like an Iron Cross.

Becca walked over and flipped the switch lowering the pair. She clipped my wrists in each cuff. The feel of the cool metal, brought comfort to my aching heart. Becca walked around to stand behind me. I heard the whip uncoil and touch the wood. She cracked it in the air. The SNAP in the air made my heart leap. Yes! That's what I needed.

"Have you been a bad boy, Jack?" she queried.

Unable to voice anything at the moment, I nodded.

She cracked the whip. It bit me on my side making me wince.

"Speak up, Jack. Have you been a bad boy?"

"Yes, Mistress," I squeaked. Why did I sound so weak? Who in the fucking hell was I? This isn't me. But I've not been me for the past couple of weeks.

"How bad, Jack?"

"Very bad. I hurt someone I love."

Silence.

This wasn't how it went. She was supposed to rapid fire questions. That's how it went. Why wasn't she asking for the count I required? My breath started to increase.

"How – how many, Jack? How many do you need?"

"Fifty. A hundred. A hundred and fifty."

"Jack—" she pleaded, again breaking protocol.

"Becca! Just do it!" I shouted.

"I will give you twenty-five." She cleared her throat. "We'll evaluate then."

I stood straight, ready for the first bite.

*   *   *

h, really, Mr. Stevens, *sir*. What else do you want to do?" Beth said, bringing me out of my head.

"Beth, I don't need that stuff—"

"But what if I do?" she asked, as serious as a heart attack. "What punishment would you deliver for me walking out on you?"

I didn't know what to say to that. Did I tell her that her walking out nearly killed me?

"I-I'm sorry," she stammered. "That day has weighed on me... the wine... I—"

I shook my head and picked up her hand. "Shhh. It's okay. Let's not talk about that."

Her phone chirped. It was a cricket sound. "Greg," she whispered. "I should go. This was a lovely lunch. I'm glad the venue will work for the photo shoot. I have to go." She scrambled to her feet and was gone in a flash.

I slammed the car door and dropped my head onto the steering wheel. *Get your shit together, Elizabeth... Beth... STOP!* The crickets sounded again. I grabbed my phone.

"Hi Greg, what's up?" I answered, faking an up beat voice.

"Jim just called. Party at their place. Giants against the Dodgers. Huge game. I told Jim you'd make your artichoke spinach dip. Cool?"

"I thought we were going out to dinner Friday?" I asked, confused. Why is he doing this? No matter what I want, it's ignored. *Jack would never shove me off like this,* I thought. It'd be dinner and theatre if I wanted.

"But it's the Giants and the Dodgers. Can we do dinner on Saturday? I'll take you Tra Vigne. We'll make it special."

I swallowed hard. I wanted to shout, *I've already been to Tra Vigne, and it was ten times more romantic that you could make it!* What do I do? *Water the grass, Elizabeth!* I scolded myself. "Saturday sounds fine."

CHAPTER 31

Knowing that the door was open, I was ready to fling it wide open. I racked my brain for a magic bullet. I was here to woo, and a-wooing I was going to do. As I walked into the lobby at the Hilton, the rack of area activities caught my eye. I scanned the pamphlets. Hundreds of vineyards aside, I spotted: balloon rides, massages, and bike rides. Just as I'd given up, I spotted a brochure for the San Francisco Ballet. *Jackpot!*

Our Lincoln Center evening blazing in my mind. Her magnificent exhibition of fellatio in the limo. My insane teasing of her during intermission while she wore that incredible Givenchy gown and those fabulous shoes… and after. I grabbed the glossy paper and scanned the calendar for what would be showing this weekend. I couldn't believe how perfect that Cinderella was opening this Friday! My mind immediately jumped to the fabulous Sergio Rossi Caged Crystal Booties.

I pulled out my phone and immediately called the ticket office. I bought a pair of orchestra seats and had arranged for them to be Fed Exed to the hotel here.

My plan: Send the tickets to Beth. Both tickets. Tell her to go with Greg and enjoy. And if he is unwilling to enjoy some beautiful theatre with a beautiful woman, I would be available.

Next, I headed into downtown Napa. I walked the quaint streets in search of a shop should Beth need a dress for the ballet. I came across this adorable shop called Une Grande Fête. The window showed a couple of elegant gowns. Not couture, but very suitable. Inside, I was greeted by an adorable older woman.

"Bonsoir, monsieur," she warmly greeted me. "Can I help you?"

I looked around the boutique and nodded. "I believe you can," I answered.

Fifteen minutes later, I had an account opened and instructions for Marie, the shop owner.

Wednesday afternoon, a package was delivered. It was a simple box with a light blue ribbon. After signing for it, I stood stunned. The last time I got a package delivered, inside was a couture gown and sensational shoes. I had taken those shoes out more than a couple of times to just look at them. I set the package on the counter and walked to the wet bar in the living room and debated wine or Scotch. Wine was civilized for two in the afternoon. Scotch seemed a little broodish. Wine was ordinary, Scotch was… Scotch was Jack. I thought better of a drink at all and grabbed a cold bottle of water, which of course made me remember Kevin. *Water the grass.*

"Shut up!" I shouted to the voices in my head.

I marched over and pulled the ribbon carefully from the box and opened it. A card sat in the box, with an envelope under it. With a trembling hand, I picked up the card. Opening it, Jack's familiar penmanship leapt off the paper.

Dearest Beth,

Friday is opening night for the San Francisco Ballet Company's performance of Cinderella. I hope you and Greg enjoy a night of theatre, and I know you have the perfect <u>slippers</u>. If you are in need of a gown (and I hope you are), I've spoken to Marie at Une Grande Fête, a boutique on Coomb Street. I have set up an account for you, if you would like to go shopping there.

Also, I have set up a full spa experience at Cleopatra's on Main Street for you and Jessica, commencing at 10am on Friday. I seem to recall that you are an early riser, so I hope that time suits you and her.

In the event Greg, or a friend, isn't available to go with you, I am free.

~Jack

My heart pounded. Jack really got me. He understood me on a level that Greg never would. But here he was telling me to go with Greg. Could he be any more enigmatic? No, I think not. I opened the ticket envelope and checked the seats. Cinderella. Ballet. San Francisco. How magical.

At dinner, with our minimal conversation, I took a shot. "You know how you want to go to the game at Jim's on Friday?"

"Yeah, can't wait," he said, finishing a bite.

"Well, I was given a pair of tickets to the San Francisco Ballet that night," I said, omitting a slight detail.

"The ballet? You're asking me to pass up Giants versus Dodgers for the ballet?"

"It's opening night. They're really great seats," I continued.

"Maybe one of your girlfriends would like to? I'm really not a theatre going kind of guy."

I thought about what he said. That he was willing to let me go to the theatre with anyone but him. Something I loved, and he couldn't give it up for one night. He was sticking to his desires instead of mine.

I nodded. "Sure, I'll ask a friend."

After dinner, I texted Jack.

> 8:45pm
> Interested in going to
> the ballet on Friday
> night? I have tickets,
> and perfect shoes.

My phone buzzed fifteen seconds later.

> 8:45pm
> It would be my
> greatest honor.
> Pick you up at 3
> for dinner in SF?

Grinning like a school girl, I texted back.

8:46pm
`That would be lovely.`
`Thank you.`

My next text was to Jessica.

8:47pm
`I'm going to do some`
`shopping downtown`
`tomorrow. Want to`
`join me? And how do`
`you feel about the spa`
`on Friday?`

She must have been busy, because I didn't get a reply for another half an hour. But she was in.

9:16pm
`Do bees buzz?`

Really? The ballet? She knew I didn't do ballet. Especially when the Giants were playing. Besides, if she's going all the way to San Francisco, I'd get another night off.

CHAPTER 32

I tossed my phone on the bed and quickly changed into workout clothes. *We're going to the theatre again!*

Punishing the hotel's gym, I ran, lifted weights, and then swam until I was exhausted. At least my personal trainer, Brian, would be impressed. Usually when I took trips out of town, my workout routine suffered. Not this week. I would have preferred working out horizontally with a particular brunette.

As I worked out, I reviewed how things had gone with Beth since Monday, and the plan for tomorrow afternoon. This past week of restraint had been brutal, hence the frequent trips to the hotel's gym. To be staying just a few miles from her and not see her every day was pure torture. I wanted to spend every minute of every day with her.

And now I get to take her to the theatre again. I couldn't believe my gamble paid off. I mean, I somehow knew that Greg wouldn't come through for Beth—again, but there was a small part of me that thought the fucker might step up. I would be the one proudly walking with her on my arm to a show. I couldn't care less about ballet, but Beth did. The way her face lit up with the story unfolding in front of her was pure inspiration. I couldn't wait to see what she would wear.

Friday would be for all the marbles. It would be our last night together. Playing it cool this week has been tough, but I wanted to show Beth that I wanted her for who she was, not simply for sex. And truthfully, I did want her for her companionship as well as her spark in bed. She was funny, kind, generous and smart. Yes, she was perfectly submissive, but she was strong—so strong.

I was going to woo like nobody's business and lay out all the cards.

Thursday, I busied myself in the business center of the hotel. I hoped that Beth was shopping for a gown, but to be honest, she could show up in yoga pants, a t-shirt, and flip-flops.

I considered how the date would go. Inspired with an idea, I headed to the quaint downtown and visited a couple of shops, searching for that just right touch to make the night magical and meaningful. I stopped in every shop that might have what I wanted, but they didn't have anything that spoke to me loud enough. I ran a quick search on my phone and found what I was looking for. And the store I wanted to get the perfect piece was about forty miles away. I hoped into my car and drove to Walnut Creek, California.

At the very special store of quintessential romantic trinkets, I found precisely what I had in mind. I paid the account, tucked the small blue box in my breast pocket, and headed back to Napa, extremely hopeful for what would unfold tomorrow evening.

Friday afternoon, by the time the limo came to collect me and then head to Beth's, I was climbing the walls. I'd been replaying every memory we'd shared both in New York and here in Napa. And the more I thought about us, I knew she was the one. That all these years, I never settled because I knew that she was out there... for me... to complete me.

The limo pulled up to her house at five minutes to three. I used the time to gather my thoughts. Even though I hadn't smoked since that first week in Becca's place thirty-some years ago, I wanted a cigarette so badly right then, I probably would have sold my soul to the devil. I was so nervous. This was it. This was my swan song. Not to mention Beth and me in a limo, our attentions undivided for over an hour as we drove to San Francisco. My mind refused to shake the memories of her on her knees giving me the most rewarding head I'd ever gotten. She wasn't the most skilled, and the way she took direction was admirable, but that she gave of herself so selflessly was truly humbling. That she gave of herself so completely made me want to be a better man.

At three o'clock sharp, I shook off the nerves and pumped myself up, buttoned up my tux, and stepped out of the car. I made my way to the door, picturing the many dresses at Une Grande Fête. Marie called late yesterday to let me know that there were charges to the account. I shook my head realizing that Beth had chosen one of the more…economical… dresses. Marie wouldn't spill about the details of the dress that Beth had chosen. She only said that Beth was *une belle femme*.

I knocked on the door and waited. My mouth was dry, my heart was pounding through my chest, and my palms were sweaty. I heard the locks on the door and stopped breathing.

When the door opened, the world dropped away. She stood in front of me, a vision in royal blue. The gown was a simple, floor-length, strapless sheath dress, a slit up her left thigh—not as high as the salmon dress, but just as sexy. The blue complimented her coloring radiantly. She wore the chocolate brown pendant, and it sparkled like her eyes. The smile that adorned her face was enough to make my heart explode. Carefully, she lifted the skirt of the dress and extended her Crystal Caged Bootie foot, for my approval. She had it. From head to toe.

"Every time I see you, I forget all the beautiful things I want to say. All I can say right now is huminah-huminah."

"Thank you," she giggled. "You don't look half bad yourself," she said running a finger on the lapel of my jacket.

"Shall we?" I asked extending my elbow.

"We shall." She turned and made sure the door was closed, and arm-in-arm we headed to the waiting limo.

The ride to ballet was a challenge. She spoke filling the silence, talking about the ballet and what she'd learned online. Her enthusiasm was rewarding. I was delighted to bring her such joy. But truth be told, I didn't hear much. Watching her lips move, coupled with her bare shoulders, and the perfume she wore, I was ready to push her down on the seat and fuck her like the animal I was, especially when she would put her hand on my knee, or let her head drop to my shoulder while she laughed.

I imagined leaning over and licking the line from the back of her ear all the way down to where her neck met her shoulder. I wanted to slip my hand into the slit of the skirt and run my hand up her inner thigh until she trembled as I reached her apex. Then I would slide down on my knees in front of her, like she had done to me on our way to the theatre just a couple weeks ago. I would spread her thighs and run my tongue along the soft, creamy skin. I would inhale her musky, salty, sweet scent and press my lips on to the heat source through her panties.

Oh, her panties… What style would she be wearing? Certainly lace. What color? I imagined hot pink. Then I imagined shifting the hot pink lace aside, licking her from the bottom of her slit up through to her clit, with an extra flick of attention at her love button. I'd clamp my lips around that sensitive nub as I slid a finger into her hot center. She'd writhe with pleasure. That mew she made when she was growing more excited would come from her throat. I'd then plunge a second finger in. I'd crook my fingers, searching for that textured spot. I'd rub, press, and suck until she flooded my mouth with her essence. And I'd lap up every drop. Then I'd kiss her deeply and let her know how good she tasted.

I was pulled out of my musings when she pushed a glass of Scotch into my hand. "You look like you could use a drink. Are you okay?" she asked. She was so good to me.

"I'm always okay when you're near," I said, sipping the brown liquid.

Her smile made my heart beat even faster.

Inside the restaurant was even more of a challenge. Watching her eat, I recalled the first day I saw her, eating that steak salad, her tongue catching the dressing at the corner of her mouth, only this time it was béarnaise sauce on filet mignon. And then, there was the matter of the small box in my pocket. My plan was to wait for the intermission of the ballet, but my heart was pounding. Maybe I should try and find a time at dinner? Or do I wait for the intermission at the ballet as planned? Or do I take her for drinks afterward? Was this whole plan a good one?

"Are you sure you're okay?" she asked interrupting my crazed thoughts.

"Me? Fine as frog's hair. Why do you ask?"

"You're just very quiet this evening, that's all," she said off handedly.

"I am simply enjoying your company, Beth. I like to listen to you. Please, continue with Carter's latest find in Pompeii."

She poured two packets of sugar into her espresso and stirred slow-ly, choosing her next words. "This has been my happiest week in California."

I looked at her confused. Her *happiest?*

"You listen to me. You get me. You do things for me that I am interested in," she stated.

My heart was banging on the inner walls of my chest. I feared I might have a heart attack. After all the working out I'd done this week, a couple remarks from the love of my life would do me in. "I've enjoyed every minute." I took her hand and rubbed my thumb over her delicate knuckles.

"I am a *little* disappointed that you've not tried to... you know," she blushed.

Oh hell! "Believe me, the thought has crossed my mind...on more than one occasion," I winked. Maybe I should have gone for broke in the limo. "But Beth, you are so much more than that to me." *Now? Was this the opportunity?*

Just then the server delivered the check, and I checked my watch. "We have to get going! We don't want to miss the first act." The box would have to wait.

I quickly paid the check and we hurried to the limo for the thankful-ly short ride to the War Memorial Opera House with no time to spare. If the ride were any longer, I would have sunk my fingers, tongue and cock into her.

CHAPTER 33

I don't know which was more magical, the dancers or the priceless expression on Beth's face with the costumes, coupled with her laughter at the comedy woven into the story. When she carefully took my hand the moment Prince Charming met Cinderella, and knew they were falling in love, I prayed this was Beth's signal to me that I was home free… Home with *my* princess. With each musical number, we got closer to the end of the first act, and I rehearsed it all in my mind.

The curtain dropped for intermission and Beth turned to me, beaming. "This is wonderful, Jack. Thank you."

"Come," I encouraged, standing and offering her my hand. She took my hand and stood with a suspicious gleam in her eye. "A cocktail for my princess," I invited.

We wiggled out of the row, and arm-in-arm we headed to the cocktail bar. I ordered her a glass of Chardonnay and a glass of Merlot for myself, since all they were selling were blended Scotches. Meandering through the lobby, and the other elegant, opening-night theatre goers, I spied a hallway with some doors.

Quickly, I whisked us down the hall, searching in earnest for a private room. Spotting one, I walked in and as calmly as I could, collected our glasses and set them on a nearby table. Once our hands were free, I turned and pinned her to the wall, at first with my eyes, and then with my body and mouth.

"You are too beautiful, and smart, and caring and beautiful to keep away from all night," I said between soft kisses to her lips, and ears, and neck, and that sweet little hollow at the base of her neck.

"You said beautiful twice," she breathed, my lips still pressed on hers.

"So I did. But then again when I'm with you, I lose most of my sensibilities. And you are *that* beautiful. Once isn't enough. Never enough." I stepped back slightly and reached into my pocket. When I pulled out the three-inch square, hallmark Tiffany blue box, Beth eyed me warily. I opened the box with the prize inside facing her. She gasped and her hand, trembling, flew to her mouth.

"Jack, I—"

I placed a finger on her luscious lips. "Shh-sh-sh. It's not what it looks like."

"It looks a lot like ring."

I glanced at the sparkling trinket. A platinum ring with a delicate infinity symbol. The symbol was fashioned with inset diamond baguettes. "Okay, it is what it looks like."

"I – I – I don't think—" she stammered.

"Hey, it's okay. It's just a promise ring. A *friendship* ring. I want you to know that you will forever be in my heart." I slipped it from the box, and placed the box in my pocket. Gently I took her right hand and slipped it on her ring finger. It fit perfectly. Together we stared at it. The lighting in the room let the piece shine and glimmer.

I looked up to see a tear in her eye. I reached for my kerchief and blotted her eyes.

"Why do I cry every time you give me jewelry?" she asked laughing nervously.

"Beth," I said with all seriousness. "You should be showered with gifts and jewelry at every opportunity. You should be treasured. You should be adored. Why are you here with me and not *him*?" That last bit was a low blow, but I couldn't help it. I searched her face for her take on it. She looked deeply into my eyes, then down at the ring.

The light flickered in the hallway catching our attention. "The intermission is over. Shall we head back in?" she whispered. *Shit!* Did I play it wrong? Too much?

"Um… sure." I extended my arm. She took a cleansing breath and took my arm. She was gripping it tightly. Nice and tight. *Tight because I'm hurting her? Tight because she wants me?* I picked up our glasses, handed Beth hers, tossed back the rest of my wine, and quietly we walked back to the theatre. Beth sipped her wine quietly. I wish I could read her mind. What was she thinking?

A ring. He got me a ring. A *Tiffany* ring. I thought when he pulled us down that hallway it was going to be a repeat of Lincoln Center. No. He gave me *forever.*

As the house lights went down and the curtain went up, I didn't notice anything on stage. There was another show playing in my head. My last few moments with Jack in New York came flooding back to me.

*   *   *

'Because I'm a selfish man who has never felt for another person what I feel for you. Because I want nothing more than to treasure you, and worship you for the next twenty or thirty years. I want to take you to Europe and South America. I want to make you feel as good about yourself as I feel about you. Because I like who I am when I'm with you." He placed his hands on my shoulders and leaned in to kiss my forehead.

His kisses trailed down my nose and across my cheek then followed my jaw. Tears filled my eyes. I bit the insides of my cheeks to keep from crying. When he pulled back and looked me in the eye, his eyes were not just filled with tears, they were flowing down his face.

My heart shattered into a million pieces. What kind of heartless bitch am I? I broke my husband's heart. I broke Kevin's heart. I was breaking Jack's heart. I had broken my own heart. The tears I'd worked at holding back, broke free. I let them stream down my face shamelessly.

His lips, trembling, came to rest on mine. His kiss was sweet. His hands gentle.

"Please?" he murmured against my lips. "Don't go."

"Jack. I have to choose, and I chose. I have to know if—"

He cut me off by kissing me, his tongue easily gaining entrance to my willing mouth.

I pushed against his strong chest. He let me.

"I won't give up on you, Beth. I can't. You are a part of me as much as I am a part of you. You can go back to Napa, but you'll always be here." He placed his hands over his heart. *"I'll wait for you. I'll wait because you're worth it."*

I leaned in and sweetly kissed the side of his mouth. I would have kissed his cheek, but that was too cold. And if I placed my lips on his, I wouldn't have left. Pulling back, I could see the sadness in his eyes, and a glimmer of hope. I swallowed, turned, and walked away.

*   *   *

I remembered standing there in his foyer, the tears…flowing, the ache in my chest…unbearable. How could I have walked away? And returned to… *this*. A life with a husband who was apparently incapable of change.

My right thumb ran over the new band on its hand, while my thumb on my left hand fidgeted with the wedding bands.

I'd come home convinced that my little planned abduction of Greg and the surprise few days would be fun, and that when we got home, I'd maybe have at least a week of a new Greg. After the lackluster stay in the hotel, his refusal of my advances, his refusal to take a dominant position, and returning to the house, it was as if I had never left. Sunday night over dinner, I'd made Chicken Parmesan, I suggested marriage counseling. He practically laughed. *You're kidding right? We're fine. We're going to be just fine*, he said. Then, on Monday, Jack showed up with an invitation to dinner. An invitation I was going to decline. But then Greg called in with a late night cancellation of dinner. Tonight, a baseball game was more important than an evening with me….

Jack had followed me to California within a week. He has been attentive and respectful. He has been doing things for me. And I had no reason to believe things would change. But then again, I've only known him for a month. This was still the honeymoon phase. He was surrounded by amazingly beautiful, young, and powerful women. His whole past was littered with women. Women who clearly wanted him. He had been a proud confirmed bachelor. Could I handle that? Could he? Would he tire of me?

What would be worse? A safe, comfortable, yet neglected life? Or a life that could end in an instant?

I was an emotional basket case. My 'lady days' had ended. Maybe hormones were still messing with my mind. I just needed a full day to clear my head.

CHAPTER 34

After the intermission, Beth was different. She kept to herself. Her constant fidgeting didn't go unnoticed. The show ended, we applauded.

"The show was... lovely," she said, a small smile on her face. But it wasn't a smile that reached her eyes.

I racked my brain with what to say. I overstepped. I had one more card to play. Silently we walked to the limo, an artificial smile on Beth's face.

We settled into the car, and the driver started off toward Napa. "Can I get you a drink?" I asked, grabbing a glass from the bar in the back of the limo.

She nodded.

"Wine or Scotch?" I offered.

"Scotch, please," she whispered. *Fuck!* If she's asking for hard stuff, she's not in a relaxed way.

I poured two Macallan's and handed her a glass. She immediately took a generous sip and let her head drop back onto the headrest.

"I'm sorry, Be—" I started, but stopped immediately when her head popped up and her eyes went wide on me.

"Don't be. I'm the one who should be sorry. You've given me this perfect night, and then I..." she let the sentence drift. *You what??* I wanted to scream. "It's just that none of this is easy."

Go for broke, Stevens. "It was easy in Manhattan. Come home with me tomorrow." I pulled a folded piece of paper from my breast pocket. "This is the info for the flight home. Private jet. Napa airport."

She carefully unfolded the paper as if it were rare and precious, her hands trembling. I popped on the light so she could read the details. "God give me strength," she sighed. "You're out of your mind."

"Do you love me? Do you feel for Greg what you *feel* for me?"

"Jack, that's not—"

"Just answer the question. Don't rationalize or listen to the voices in your head. Listen to your heart. Do you love me?"

She stared deeply into my eyes. "Yes, Jack." My breathing quickened. I wanted to hear her say it. I wanted to hear those words. I willed her to say them. "I love you." I crashed my lips to hers and consumed her, while she kissed me back, pound-for-pound what I gave her. I pulled her into me and hugged her tightly.

"But—"

"No *buts,* Beth," I said pushing her back and leveling her with my eyes. "Love is all you need."

"Did you just quote the Beatles?"

"I guess I did. But it's true."

"Can I think about it?" she asked.

I looked at my watch. "The plane leaves in about twelve hours."

We fell into a silence. It wasn't a comfortable one, but it wasn't exactly strained. She was processing.

"I have a confession to make. A couple of confessions, actually," I said

"Uh-oh. Should I be nervous?" she asked.

"When you left, you broke my heart."

Her face fell, and she was quiet. She looked up at me, her eyes brimming with tears. "I'm sorry."

"I got rip roaring drunk and spent three days in a stupor."

"Jack—"

"I'm not telling you this for pity, just, Becca found me and sobered me up."

"She's a good friend, you're very lucky."

"She told me to come here to you. She told me to come and get my heart back. Beth," I searched her eyes to see if she was hearing me. She was. "You are my heart. You're what makes it tick. You're the missing piece. When I'm with you, I feel at peace. When I'm with you, I feel like things make sense. Before I met you, I was meandering through life. I never understood why people got married. I had meaningless flings and did what I could to make it through the next day. But the day you came into my life, I looked forward to getting up and making it through the day to see you. I had fun planning things to do with you. I finally got it. I understood why people got married. I understood what they were talking about when they would drone on about how their guy or girl made them feel. Am I making sense?"

She nodded and closed her eyes. A tear streamed down her face.

"Hey, I didn't mean to make you cry. I'm sorry. I just wanted to say my piece while you consider your next move." I cupped her adorable face, and brushed the tear away with my thumb.

"You continually surprise me," she said covering my hand with hers. "You say the most beautiful things, and—"

"And?" *And you already said you love me. You've decided? You've chosen me?*

"I have so much to think about," she sighed, sliding down in her seat and tucking herself under my arm. I pulled her in close and relished the contact. I tried recording in my brain every detail about her. Her scents, her sounds, her taste...

We drove home in quiet, holding hands. He really was the sweetest thing. I couldn't believe my luck, or my curse, that we'd come together. I couldn't believe that he was leaving tomorrow. I couldn't believe I was holding an opportunity to fly back with him. I wanted so desperately to just say, *Fuck it,* and pack all my stuff and meet him on that plane. But I had come home for a reason, although I really couldn't remember why any more.

I stepped into the house feeling overwhelmed. Leaving Jack in the limo, I couldn't bring myself to say goodbye, or see you later. I didn't say anything. I didn't know how I felt. I did, but it was a horrible feeling. I opened my clutch and looked at the itinerary Jack had given me. Looking at the clock and seeing it was twelve thirty, I realized that Jack's flight was set to leave in less than twelve hours. I slipped off my Cinderella slippers and set them carefully at the hallway to the bedroom, and walked over to the kitchen to pour myself a drink.

Rummaging through the bottles, I found the bottle of Glenfiddich 18 that Greg had received a couple of years ago from his company when he landed the Franklin Complex account. I don't know why, but I smiled when I noticed that the seal had not yet been broken. I broke the seal and opened the bottle. Pouring a single, then changing my mind, I poured a double. Lifting the glass to my nose, I took in the aroma that was absolutely Jack in my mind.

I walked through the living room and looked around at my life. I had raised three wonderful kids here, and those memories were in every corner. I looked at the dining table, recalling the birthday parties, puzzles, and school projects. In the TV room, I saw movie nights with the kids, and the kids with their friends. But looking around I didn't see memories of me and Greg. Even after the kids were gone. I saw Greg typing away for hours in the office, or seated with his laptop with CNN or Headline news on the TV, but not him active with the family, or with me.

I sipped the Scotch, and let it warm me as I stepped outside onto the patio in the cool spring evening. I couldn't quite grasp how I felt. Is love all we need? Will that be enough? Greg was safe. He wasn't going anywhere. He didn't care if I came (even in bed) or went, as long as I was there to pick up his dry cleaning, keep the house tidy, go with him as his little trophy to parties and sports things, and make him dinner, he was fine. I could go about doing things that made me happy. The one concession he had granted me was that I could work, doing whatever I wanted.

Being put on the spot with Jack tonight and admitting that I love him – whew! It was true. I did love him. Very much so. Since the first time I saw him at Ed Scott's, I was drawn to him. Terrified by how he made me feel, but drawn nonetheless. I felt horrible when he told me that my leaving sent him into a drunken oblivion. But I knew just how he felt.

The last four weeks have been a crazy mishmash of heaven and hell. A roller coaster. I left Napa feeling like a nobody, and in New York, I felt alive. Then back to Napa and felt neglected again. Until Monday... When Jack arrived.

But could one week home undo the three I had been away? Was I giving up too quickly? Maybe therapy? Greg was nearly upset and angry when I suggested it at dinner last week. Do I try and keep watering what seemed like a dead lawn?

I sat and sipped my Scotch, recalling the past eight hours with Jack and how magical it all seemed. It was so much more than nice. The excitement, the surprise. But I'd only known Jack for a month now. Who was to say he wouldn't get bored and, now that he's decided he wants a stable relationship, he won't find someone better than me? I'm no major catch. He sees women every day who are far better looking and more fit than I am. He's in an industry that is all about looks and appearances.

But back to Greg. Twenty-four years was hard to toss away. There was something comforting knowing that Greg wouldn't leave, that he welcomed me back after my "stunt," as he called it, running to New York to figure out my mind. And there were the kids. Yes, they were all out of the house, and mature enough to understand that relationships sometimes don't work out, no matter how long you are together.

Could I handle another twenty-four years of mediocre? Did I deserve anything better? I'd run – chucked everything and didn't give any thought to leaving Greg, then just came back expecting things to be drastically improved. Greg is refusing couples counseling, so how can we improve when he doesn't listen to me?

I thought about both Jack and Greg. But the more I tried to think, the more muddled my mind became. How do you compare the two? Heart? Or head? Love? Or safe? Which factors mattered more? I thought about the lists I used to make in high school with the pros in one column and the cons in the other. I would give point values to each element and come up with a score. Well, I wasn't going to go grab paper, but I tried to come up with the thoughts I would put in a column.

Greg made me feel comfortable. Safe. He was predictable. I knew what to expect. There were no surprises. But there wasn't any heat, or fire, or passion, or excitement.

Jack made me feel all those things and then some. He made me feel special, treasured, and important. He was anything but predictable, but that was a good thing.

How could I sort this out?

I was away from Jack not one week and he was jetting across the country to see me, and fight for me. I had been in New York for almost three weeks before Greg came out.

Even after I had come back from New York, Greg was still absent, and still not what I needed. Sure, we'd had Wednesday, Thursday, and Friday night at the hotel, but things were still, as the *Fifty* book put it, vanilla. And home Saturday night? Sunday night? I was an afterthought. Greg had been focused on his files. Not me. Did that make me selfish? Maybe. But I'd been gone for three weeks and he didn't seem to be over the moon that I'd come home. He almost acted like it was expected that I would come back. And I felt like I had gone back to being a maid. When we got home on Saturday, he was all about me going grocery shopping and what's for dinner. I felt a little slutty that I wanted sex more than he did, but I now knew that men still had sex drives in their fifties.

I thought about the two philosophies. The one Shelby cited, Johnny Depp's *"If you love two people at the same time, choose the second. Because if you really loved the first one, you wouldn't have fallen for the second."* And Kevin's *abuela's* favorite, *The grass is always greener where you water it.* I'd come home to water the grass, and I felt like I was still in a field of weeds. Like the spontaneous trip to the hotel didn't matter. That the dinners I'd cooked since coming home were typical. He still wasn't paying attention to me. One would think that if your wife up and leaves you because she felt neglected, you'd stop neglecting her.

I looked over at the window that lead to our bedroom. The light was on. Greg had waited up for me. That was nice. *One last chance to water the grass*, I said to myself, thinking about the itinerary in my clutch.

I finished my Scotch and headed back inside. I set up the coffee maker then headed to the bedroom. My heart dropped. Greg was asleep, only my bedside light was on. He hadn't waited up after all.

I went to the bathroom, slipped out of my gorgeous new dress, carefully hanging it on the hanger and changed into pajamas. Staring in the mirror as I brushed my teeth and washed my face, I continued to battle with safe and comfortable or alive and daring.

I slipped into bed and gave Greg a quick kiss on the cheek. He stirred and his eyes opened. I held my breath wondering what he would say. Would he ask me about the ballet? About who I went with? Or would he tell me about the game on TV I'd missed at Jim and Jess'?

"Oh good, you're home," he said groggily. "By the way, Aaron and I have a seven-thirty tee-time tomorrow morning. Enjoy sleeping in." He kissed the air and snuggled back into his pillow.

CHAPTER 35

I returned to the Hilton deflated and exhausted. I had played every card I had. Was it enough? Would love conquer all? Or was the risk too much for her? How do I make her feel safe? And cherished? I cursed myself for staying away from serious relationships my whole adult life. If I had opened myself a little, if I hadn't let my failed relationship with Kari harden my heart all those years ago, I might have had an idea of what to do. How to do this right.

Becca and Rita had it so easy. They gave each other space and respect. I thought that was what I was doing. I absolutely respected her. I could have pressured her into my bed; I had no doubt she wouldn't need too much coaxing. From seeing her on Monday, Tuesday, and tonight, I got a clear feeling that she wanted it as much as I did. But I wanted to give her the space, the comfort… to show her that I wanted her for more than her body.

I tossed and turned all night. I didn't get any sleep. I finally crawled out of bed at five and packed my clothes. I wanted to hit the gym one last time, but was so nervous that I didn't have it in me. Would she show at the airport? Would I go home with my heart? I drove to the car rental place in a fog, returned the car, and took the shuttle to the airport where the private jet was already waiting. I looked at my watch, remembering the last time when every minute seemed to matter. The day that Elizabeth walked out.

I waited in the terminal for her. I did whatever I could to distract myself. Thumbed through magazines that were months old. Drank shit coffee from the vending machine. Even struck up a chat with the small family that sat waiting for their own plane.

Finally, a uniformed man approached me. "Mr. Stevens. I'm Adam, your attendant for your flight to JFK. We will be departing in fifteen minutes." He looked around quickly. "Have plans changed? The itinerary states that there are two travelers."

I scanned the terminal. No sign of Beth anywhere.

I laughed nervously. "You know women. Five minutes? Can we wait for five more minutes?" I pleaded. I pulled out my cell and texted Beth.

> 11:45am
> I am boarding the
> plane now. Should I
> have them hold the
> flight plan?

"I will message the captain." He pulled out his phone as well and started tapping away.

Once again, I was a slave to the clock. I watched it like a hawk. Before I knew it, five minutes had passed.

"Mr. Stevens, the captain has informed me that we cannot wait any longer, or the flight will have to refile a flight plan which will cause a considerable delay."

I looked at my cell. No reply. Should I pay an arm and a leg and reschedule the flight and insist we wait? Or did I have my answer?

I opened one eye and looked at the clock. It was seven forty-three. Greg was on the links. I remembered how he grumbled last weekend about missing his round last weekend during our "romantic" getaway. I stretched, enjoying the full space of the queen sized bed and rubbed the sleep from my eyes, contemplating my final thoughts of last night, or early this morning, however you want to look at it.

I climbed out of bed and got busy. Very busy. Around eleven, my phone chirped with a text. Glancing at the screen I saw it was from Greg. I think I actually growled when I read the message:

```
11:23
On my way. Can
you make me one
of your famous
BBQ Chicken
sandwiches for me
for lunch? Be home
in 5. Thx XOG
```

Oh, really? 'XOG' was a departure from his 'G.' signature. Why he liked to sign texts anyway, I would never know. But some things never change. He was still texting me lunch orders and errands. I smiled to myself, powered down my phone so I couldn't get anymore annoying texts, and set the phone aside finishing the last of my *ToDo List*.

I was sitting on the back patio sipping a glass of chardonnay when I heard the door open. Casually I walked into the kitchen and saw Greg standing at the fridge. He pulled out a beer and popped the top off. "Hey, there you are. Are you okay? I don't see the sandwich. That's okay. I'll make something. You must be tired from getting in so late last night. But wow! You missed quite a game. Giants lost by one run. It was brutal."

"I'm in the wrong place," I said.

"I'm sorry, what?" he said, taking a long pull off of his microbrew beer.

I cleared my throat and tried again. "I don't belong here."

"You're not making any sense, Bets. What is going on?"

"We're fooling ourselves, Greg. Do you really want to live the next twenty or thirty years like this? Predictable. Boring. Separate? You going to baseball games and golfing, me going to ballet and opera. I don't. I don't want to get texts telling me to pick up dry cleaning or make a sandwich. I don't want to feel like an afterthought," I fired off, feeling my confidence grow.

Greg looked as white as a ghost. "Elizabeth, you're scaring me. What are you trying to say?"

"I'm trying to say, that you don't want to be married to me."

"Of course I do. We took vows. Sacred vows. *Til death do us part.*"

I shook my head. "We *are* dead, Greg. You like the idea of being married to me. But you don't want to be married to me. You have no idea who I am." I finished off my glass of wine and set it in the sink. "Did we never have true love, Greg?"

"I absolutely love you!" he said raising his voice.

"Do you know how I got the tickets to Cinderella? Do you know who I went with? Do you care? You never asked. You just shrugged and didn't want to go. I've been to a hundred boring games with you. I got excited when your team was winning and annoyed when your team was losing. As for work, you're already calling off dinner at home for files and take out at work. You didn't even come home until after I was long asleep. I'd had a rough day, taking Jessica to the doctor."

"Oh, right. She said yesterday that everything looked good. That's terrific."

"You didn't even ask about her all week. This isn't right. This doesn't feel good. I'm not happy. You laughed when I suggested counseling last weekend. You're not willing to try and make changes on your own. And I'm not willing to settle. I came back to water the grass, but I don't think there's any grass left to water."

"Don't be absurd! For better or for worse, right?" he nearly shouted, throwing more vows my way. "Why do you think I went to New York to get you?"

I had to laugh at that. "When you'd come to New York, I thought *Hey! He cared enough to come after me. And he tried something new! He's capable of change.* But from the moment I came back, we were the same. We were boring. There's no spark. No chemistry. Not when I showed up at your office in lace, not in the hotel suite, and certainly not at home. I need chemistry. I need to be important enough for you to want to do stuff with me. I need to be special enough that you would wait up for me. I need to be treasured enough that you want to spend your hours not in the office, but with me, not with your files or baseball, or football or any other sport in season."

He didn't say anything. He just stood there, running his fingers through his sandy blonde hair, looking all over the place like he'd find an answer just laying around. And then he spotted my suitcases. His eyes flew to me.

"You're going back to New York to that Jack guy, aren't you?" he seethed. "It's not real with him. He's a player. He'll dump you, and don't think you will be able to come crawling back to me again," he continued. I silently thanked him for making this so much easier and thumbed the infinity ring on my right hand.

I glanced at my watch. Eleven forty. I had to get going if I was going to make it to the airport in time for the twelve fifteen flight. The itinerary said to arrive fifteen minutes before the flight and the airport was only twenty minutes away.

"Last time, I left you a letter and just left. A letter that called you perfect, which wasn't right. You are wrong when it comes to me. We aren't good. We don't work. I'm not willing to spend the next twenty or thirty years in a loveless marriage, with someone who isn't willing to work for it. No letter this time. No lies." I stuffed my hand in my pocket and pulled out the wedding rings. I walked up to him, and taking his hand, placed them carefully in his hand. "Maybe there is someone who will light you up. Someone you will want to be *with*." I kissed him on the cheek. "I'll have an attorney contact you." I turned, grabbed my suitcases, and left.

I jangled the rings in my hand and stared at the door. Well, at least this time she didn't leave a letter.

Was I hurt? Angry? Sad?

All I knew was that I was alone—again.

The bitter part of me, hoped that Elizabeth would soon find herself alone.

I never figured that she'd leave…really leave. When we met in college, she was needy and wanted to be attached. It was perfect. She was beautiful and malleable. I'd had things just how I wanted them. She kept the house neat, and running smoothly. She made amazing children that I could brag about. And I had a beautiful woman on my arm when I wanted.

We didn't have what Jess and Jim had, but what we had worked. Right? When she comes back, will I take her back? Maybe. How could I find another woman like Elizabeth? The *old* Elizabeth?

CHAPTER 36

"Mr. Stevens, please buckle up. We're just waiting to be cleared for take off," Adam said, glancing sadly at the vacant seat next to me.

I looked at my phone again to see if she texted back. Still no reply. I set the phone aside and buckled the seat belt. I listened to the engines wind up and looked out of the window. I tried to console myself that I had done everything possible to win her back. But, my years of bachelorhood failed me. They had made me into an unlovable person. I choked back the tears that threatened. I didn't deserve to cry. I had done this to myself. I tapped my foot eager for the plane to take off and get me back to New York.

Suddenly, the engines quieted. The cabin phone for the attendant rang, probably to alert Adam that our flight plan was revoked, and that I'd be stuck here for another few hours. Adam glanced at me and shot me a smile. Was it a real smile? Or an apology smile? I couldn't even tell anymore. I thought I could read people. Apparently, I was wrong. I thought I knew where Beth was, and I missed the mark there.

Adam went to the door and started to unlock it. I looked out of the window and saw a security car racing toward the plane. *What now? Was my pilot suddenly tagged for being drunk or something?*

The car came to a screeching halt and my heart stopped. Or should I say it started to beat again. Stepping out of the car was my Beth. My Breath. I quickly unlatched my belt and raced to the door. I flew down the stairs, and pulled Beth into me. I planted kisses all over her face and neck. I could hardly believe she was real. I feared that I would wake up and realize that this was some sort of sick hallucination my brain had concocted to save my sanity. I inhaled her hair, smelling the rosemary and mint. I felt the soft, supple skin of her neck. I mashed my mouth to hers and roughly parted her receptive lips, my tongue brushing over hers. No. This was real.

"I'm sorry, I'm la—"

"Don't apologize. I should have had more faith and made the captain wait at the gate. I just thought…"

"I beg your pardon, Mr. Stevens, Miss…

"Ms. Morris," she replied strongly. I looked at her with surprise. She smiled back.

"Very good, Mr. Stevens, Ms. Morris, we are still in line to take off and we're next. If we don't want to have to file a new flight plan, we'll have to get seated right away."

"Of course! Of course!" I belted with joy, not recognizing my own voice. I grabbed Beth *Morris's* bags and I followed her up the stairs.

Adam busied himself with storing the suitcases as we took our seats, Beth to the left of me, and we buckled up. I took hold of her right and noticed that she was still wearing the ring I had given her last night. I also noticed that her left hand was void of any jewelry. *Ms. Morris,* I thought to myself. She was free. She was mine.

We were quickly cleared for takeoff and while we taxied down the runway, I leaned over and kissed her deeply. I felt my heart, my whole heart, pound. This was so right.

The first hour of the flight, I simply sat back and held Beth's hand and scolded myself for not believing enough in what we had. As much as I wanted to know what she said when she left Greg, I felt it was best that we leave him back in Napa.

I shared with Beth all of the charities JSS works with, and suggested a few that she might enjoy serving on the board for. I loved watching her get excited over the possibility of working with the models and raising money for worthwhile causes. She said she'd like to go back and work at the bar a couple days a week, too—for the lunch shifts. As much as I didn't want her surrounded by other men looking at her, I wanted her to do what made her happy. And, I'd get to see her there for lunches.

Suddenly she tensed. I turned and looked at her with concern.

"What's wrong?" I asked. "Anything that is left behind, I'll make sure you get it back."

"No, I think I packed everything I needed. But I just realized, I'll be sharing an apartment with my daughter. She moves to Manhattan next week to start her internship."

"It's no problem whatsoever," I said. "You'll be staying with me."

"Jack, that isn't—"

"That isn't up for negotiation. Phoebe needs her independence, and I don't want to spend another day—or night—without you. The subject is closed." I watched her consider what I'd just said.

"We'll see..." she said back, coyly.

"No, what we'll see about is how many times you can get your Mile-High Club card punched on this flight in the room in back. We have six and half hours," he said with a hungry gleam in his eye.

When we reached cruising altitude, Adam commenced with the services the private company provided, serving us wine, along with a light cheese and cracker with fruit course. Half way through though, I couldn't take it anymore. The way Beth collected an errant crumb with her tongue, or sucked on her finger when a smudge of brie had landed there...she was doing it on purpose. Of that, I was certain.

Noting that Adam was busy in the galley, I reached over and un-buckled Beth from the seat. She started to protest, but I silenced her with a kiss. I landed a trail of kisses to her ear and growled, "Rule one of the Mile High Club: Always wear a skirt." There were no rules that I knew of, I was just having fun.

She glanced down at her pants and whispered back, "Is that a pun-ishable infraction?" Her voice was hoarse. She was as aroused as I was. *I knew her eating antics were for show.* I nodded. "What are some of the other rules?" she asked quietly.

"Rule Two: Take advantage of distracted attendants." I stood, tugged her hand, and lead her to the small bedroom at the back of the plane. We could have easily walked there whether Adam was looking or not, but it was much more fun this way.

"Rule Three," I started, grabbing at her and pushing her up against the wall, dipping my head to kiss the hollow at the base of her neck. "You must remain absolutely silent."

I looked up at her. She nodded, her eyes smoldering, her teeth trapping her lush bottom lip. I crushed that mouth with my own, taking her bottom lip between my own teeth as my hand went to work on the button and zipper of her capri pants. I slipped my hands into the waistband and in the back, grabbing her tight ass and pulling her into my raging hard-on. *She must work out,* I thought, as I noted how firm it really was. For a moment I wondered what it would be like to workout along side her, and I couldn't wait to get her into the gym.

She mewed into my mouth as I squeezed one cheek, and ran a finger along the crack of her ass with my other hand. Briefly, I considered taking her ass on the plane, but ruled against it. I wanted to hear her when I sunk myself into that tight place.

I slid her pants and panties down and off along with her sandals. Her careful leg and pussy landscaping did not go unnoticed. I spent a good long moment stroking the skin that was as smooth as silk, and her pussy nicely trimmed. I ran my nose up her inner thigh and inhaled, taking in her delicious musky scent. I felt her knees tremble slightly. *Oh, this is going to be fun.*

As I sat back on the bed, she leaned against the wall, bare from the waist down, wearing just a lovely sleeveless, plum colored top. "Take it off." I ordered. Her hands slowly went to the top button and she started to undo each of them one by one, teasing. Too slowly. By the time she reached the second button, my already hard cock was pulsing madly. I was almost afraid of moving for fear of shooting off my load. I'd done nothing but my hand for the past week, and with Beth inches from me, stripping, I was nearing my wits end. I stood quickly and grabbed the button edges of her shirt firmly.

"Rule Four," I stated. "Move quickly." I ripped the shirt open, sending the last few buttons flying. She let out the breath she was holding in, and as it washed over it intoxicated me even more. I slid my hands up her sides and took her covered breasts into my palms. I rubbed my thumbs over her nipples and felt how taut they were. I dropped my head to her left breast, took her lace-covered mound in my mouth and drew my teeth to her nipple, then bit gently. She gasped and trembled.

As my body pressed against hers, I debated. Do I fuck her against the wall? Or do we use the bed?

Yes, I wanted to fuck her, but more than that, I wanted to make love to her. Yes, I'd be violating my own made up rule to "move quickly," but hey—rules are made to be broken. I wrapped my arms around her and planted my mouth on hers, plunging my tongue into her mouth. She responded just as lustily. I lifted her and turned us, so that she was backed up to the bed, then slowly lowered her.

I stood and let my eyes take in her incredible body. My eyes rested on her triangle, and I knew what I needed next. "Scoot," I ordered, my eyes darting to the head of the bed. She obeyed quickly, honoring Made-Up Rule Four. *God she was amazing!*

The temperature in the room having risen at least fifteen degrees, I unbuttoned my linen shirt and slid it off, tossing it onto Beth's pile of clothes. Her eyes were tracking my every move. Enjoying her attention, I unbuckled my belt and slid it from the loops. Bending the belt in half, I snapped it a few times, causing it to crack loudly. Her eyes flew wide. I waggled my brow, smirked, and tossed the belt aside. I dropped my pants and kicked them aside. I stood proudly in front of Beth, my cock jutting out nobly in front of me, enjoying Beth's appraisal as much as I was.

I stepped forward and placed my hands on her ankles, slowly moving them up to her knees, then spread her legs wide. I knelt between her and slowly lapped at her slit from bottom to top with a wide tongue, noting that she was well and truly wet. I loved how she tasted, a mix of tart, sweet and salty. I couldn't get enough of it. And as she writhed under me, I clamped my mouth on her clit and slipped two fingers into her wet quim. I started to stroke that front wall and, before long, her walls were rhythmically clamping around my fingers. Strangled cries came from her throat. My love was abiding by Fake Rule Number Three.

I slid up and kissed her deeply, while rubbing my dick along her slit. She eagerly kissed me back, tilting her hips up to me, trying to grind on my member.

She slid a hand between us and lined up the engorged head to that velvety spot. I pulled my head back and looked at her.

"What? You said move quickly. So hurry up!" She grinned from ear-to-ear.

Without wasting another moment, I sunk into her—full hilt. Another strangled cry, and she bit down on her lip to keep from crying out. And if I hadn't been looking into her eyes, I might have worried. But her eyes were aflame with passion and need. Her hands flew to my back and she dug her nails in. My heart started pounding dangerously, and I was coming unhinged. That combination of pain and pleasure.

"Keep that up, baby. I love your nails," I grunted. She firmly dragged them toward my ass as I slid nearly out, then plunged back in deeply, quickly, and almost roughly.

Suddenly the plane dropped and bounced with turbulence, as Beth gripped me tighter, her nails probably drawing blood. I exploded, finding my release.

I collapsed on top of her, panting. The plane still bobbing and lurching. "Welcome to the Mile High Club," I breathed.

Kissing on takeoff was quite exhilarating. Of course, I could kiss Jack at a landfill, or in a Manhattan subway station, and still feel the same rush. And this time, the kiss was so much sweeter.

But sex on a plane? Now *that* was the pinnacle of pleasure. As I lay in Jack's arms, I considered the intense coupling we just had. It wasn't just that we could have been 'caught' by the attendant at any moment, or that Jack knew just how to wind me up, although that was a close call. Most of all, it was the first time with Jack when I felt completely free. I had completely let go. I was his completely.

EPILOGUE

He fought tooth and nail, but in the end, Jack won, and that's what mattered. Beth moved in with him. She had insisted on taking the guest room, but she spent most nights in Jack's room. He loved the way his bed smelled of her.

Beth served Greg with divorce papers just two days after returning to Manhattan. Without contesting it, their divorce could be finalized in a matter of weeks. Beth used Jack's attorney, and received no indication from Greg's attorney that Greg was going to put up a fight. Beth asked for nothing. No furnishings, or items of any sentimental value. Anything she wanted, she'd packed when she left. Everything else was tainted. The kids were adults, so no custody issues there. And financially, Beth's money, namely her inheritance, had been properly managed. Greg had no way of touching it. Beth's financial independence wasn't necessary though, because it was Jack's greatest honor to provide everything for her. But Beth had her pride, and Jack let her have it.

Beth went back to Ed Scott's and easily got her job back. Three lunch shifts a week. She finally started bartending classes and began her certification. Additionally, she went to work for JSS, serving on the board for two charities, a literacy campaign and their grandest fundraiser, one raising money for breast cancer research.

The most incredible part was taking her to East Fifty-first Street. They had gone to dinner with Becca and Rita. Everyone got along famously. They all chatted easily and freely. Leaving the restaurant, Jack and Beth decided to walk, as the early May evening was unseasonably warm.

"Tell me something," she said, tucked under Jack's protective arm.

"I love you, and I can't wait to get home and do unsavory things to you. That kind of something?" he growled in her ear, knowing she'd be willing. He imagined she was already soaking her panties. The way she had been rubbing her foot up and down his leg all throughout dinner, Jack knew full well she was in a frisky mood.

"Well, always, but…what's at Fifty-first Street?" Becca had leaned over to Rita after Rita made a cheeky remark and said *'Do I have to take you to Fifty-first Street?'* Jack hoped Beth hadn't heard that, but apparently her hearing was as good as ever. It wasn't that he didn't want to take Beth to his private place, his first apartment, his 'dungeon,' but he wanted to make sure that Beth was fully prepared for what she would see there.

These past two weeks, post-Napa time, and here in Manhattan, had been incredible. Beth's willingness and sexual freedom were more than Jack expected. *Could she handle more?* he wondered. "Maybe I'll show you one day," Jack said instead.

"Or you'll show me now," she said stopping in her tracks. She held out her arm to hail a cab as if she'd lived here her whole life. One quickly stopped and she dragged Jack to the waiting yellow car.

Inside, Jack told the driver, "Thirty-eighth and Thir—"

"No!" she interrupted. "Fifty-first Street."

"It'll be a long walk home from there, Sweetheart, but if it's a long walk you're after, I'm all too happy to oblige."

"You'll show me what's at Fifty-first."

"And what if Fifty-first is occupied? Becca and Rita may be there."

She pouted. God, how Jack wanted to suck on that plump lower lip. His cock throbbed it's own desire. "Text her and find out. I want to know," she whined "And you'll show me or I may be the one flogging and taking a crop to you." Jack's afore mentioned cock leapt to attention. If Beth wanted to see East Fifty-first, Jack was going to show her. He texted B asking if she was taking R there tonight. His answer arrived in just a couple seconds.

10:47pm
Not tonight. ;]

Beth, having seen the incoming text, nudged Jack, who gave the cabbie the new address, and off they went. "East Fifty-first was my first apartment," he told her.

"You still have it? That's cute. But isn't your bachelor pad on Thirty-Eighth enough?"

"We'll see how cute it is when I show you the place." Before Jack knew it, they were outside the door to his first apartment.

He took a deep breath as they stood outside the door. "I'm sorry. You don't have to show me, if you don't want to," she said, taking his hand.

"No, I want to. I think you might enjoy this."

She raised her brows at him, as he slid the key in, and opened the door. They stepped in carefully and Jack flipped the switch on. The soft light illuminated his private lair. Carefully, he watched Beth's reaction. Her eyes carefully scanned the walls, the walls that were decorated with paddles, crops, and whips. Handcuffs of all kinds: silver, fuzzy, and medieval. Packaged dildos, plugs, and beads. Various sized spreaders, a large St. Andrew's Cross and a small Wartenberg wheel.

She walked by the furnishings, which weren't many. He could only guess at what she was thinking, while she took in the spanking bench, the Berkley Horse and the sex swing. Not all items were Jack's purchases. B and R actually outfitted most of what was found here.

She made her way back to the spanking bench, and locked eyes with Jack. Slowly she leaned over it and rested on the platform with an inquisitive, "Hm-mmm." Her eyes growing hooded, she slowly pulled up her skirt higher and higher. As the hem reached her ass, then over her backside, Jack almost shot a load. He bit his lip and read her face. Standing straighter, and not breaking eye contact, he walked to the wall. He fingered the whips, cuffs, and packaged goodies. Her eyes flicked to the floggers and a smile spread on both of their faces.

He pulled a lovely leather, not suede, one from the wall and swaggered over to her at the bench. He stood commandingly at her head. With an almost drunken grin, she looked up at him. The good girl that she was, and how she knew him so well, she waited for his command.

"Take out my cock," he breathed.

"Yesss, Sirrr," she slurred coyly. She reached for his slacks and un-zipped the fly, then finagled his straining member from his boxers. She waited, panting, lips parted and lush. Jack had been a Dom for many years, but no one drove him as insane as Beth did. He strained to control himself. Every time she touched him, breathed on him, or even looked at him, he almost came.

"Take it in as deeply as you can."

"Yesss, Sirrr," she purred. He slid his dick into her mouth until his pubes were touching her nose. Anywhere, this would drive him crazy, but here, in *this* place, with *Beth*, his *breath*, he was quickly losing his mind.

She worked his cock as she'd learned to do over the past couple of weeks. She was perfect, and got better every time. She swirled her tongue over his pulsing crown, then slid down the shaft slowly until he was pushed against the back of her throat. He reached forward and rubbed his hands over her ass, massaging and dragged my nails across the skin, creating small, pink tracks. She moaned with every stroke.

He pulled out of her, wanting this little game to go on a little longer, and if he stayed seated in her mouth, he was going to blow. He wanted to explode in her glorious pussy, not her mouth. He walked around to her back side, his cock bobbing proudly in front of him while admiring the designs he'd clawed.

"Have you been a good girl? Or a bad girl?" he asked, slapping the flogger in his hand. He'd not yet introduced her to this game and he eagerly awaited her reply.

"I've been good, Sir," she replied.

Hmm. That answer doesn't work in my game, he thought. He changed his question.

"So why are you here?" he asked, looking forward to this reply.

"Because I love the flogger," she breathed.

Okay then, he thought. *I can work with that.*

He commenced with the flogging her ass, listening to her groan with pleasure. As her rear grew to a deep pink, he noticed fluid running down her thigh. He stopped the flogging.

"Are you aroused, Breath?" he asked, using his nickname for her.

"Beyond, Sir," she replied, her voice trembling.

"What would you like me to do about it?" he queried, his own passion consuming him.

"Fuck me, Sir," she groaned.

Instantly, he dropped the flogger and lined up behind her. In one thrust, he was balls deep in her fiery core. She grunted, as he hit her deepest center. Jack was not unfamiliar with that sound from her. Sweat broke out on his brow. Thank God she was so close because he needed to come. He needed to come deeply inside her. With four, maybe five rough thrusts, she quivered around his cock and milked his own climax from him.

He collapsed on top of her back, panting heavily. "I love you, Beth," he breathed on her neck.

"I love you, too, Jack."

He never knew he would be so happy. So complete. Not in his wildest dreams.

~~~THE END~~~

Chasing The Dream
Book 3 in the Dream Series
Fall 2014

Phoebe Fairchild didn't have a great first year of college. In fact, it stunk! She realized she'd chosen a major, Physics, that didn't suit her. And worse than that, a boyfriend who was a first-class jerk.

When she visited her mother in New York for Spring Break, Phoebe decided that a transfer to a new university, a thousand miles from her current one, and a new major were definitely in order. With a little assistance from her mother's friend, Jack Stevens, Phoebe worked a transfer to NYU and an internship at a major TV network.

Phoebe moved into her mother's old apartment and, with her super sexy neighbor, Kevin Parker, figured out The Big Apple. But the biggest challenge was to be her internship assignment: Personal Assistant to mega star, Chase Smythe. Since she was nine years old, Phoebe had been starry-eyed for the blond haired, blue eyed actor. Her room had been practically wallpapered in Chase Smythe pullouts from the teen magazines.

But Chase Smythe wasn't the charming, sexy actor on TV and in the movies he starred in, or how he behaved in interviews. No. Seemed that over the years, stardom had jaded him. In real life, Chase was full of himself, lazy and left a path of destruction in his wake that had been well concealed by his former 'handlers.' Now it was Phoebe's job to reign him in.

Nonetheless, there is a spark. Phoebe was warned to not cave into his charms, as fake as they are, but there's more than just his charm. There's chemistry. Is it real? Or is it an act? Will Chase let Phoebe in to see the real person, not the just TV personality?

Trademark Acknowledgment

I acknowledge the use of the following registered names, trademarks, etc. I have not received any compensation for using these names. No copyright infringement is intended:

ABBA, Adidas, *Alice*, Ansonia Motel, Ava Gabor, Bain de Soleil, Barbie, The Beatles, The BeeGees, Ben-Gay, Brooklyn Bridge, Budweiser, *Cats!*, Chanel No. 5, Chanel Mademoiselle, Chevrolet, Cinderella, Claudia Schiffer, CNN/Headline News, Columbia University, Corvette, *Cosmopolitan Magazine*, Cracker Jacks, Daisy Duke, *The Dating Game*, David Gandy, Donna Summer (titles: *Hot Stuff* and *Bad Girls*), *The Dukes of Hazzard*, Embassy Suites, Empire State Building, FedEx, Ford Automobiles, Fordham University, Ford Modeling, San Francisco Ballet Company, San Francisco Giants, *Green Acres, Glamour Magazine*, Glenfiddich, Guess! Jeans, Hilton Hotels, *The Incredible Hulk*, iPhone, Jack Daniels, Jim Lange, Johnny Paycheck (title: *Take This Job and Shove it!*), John Travolta, Kiss (title: *Love 'Em and Leave 'Em*), L.A. Dodgers, Le Coutume Café, Lexus, Lincoln Center, Lone Ranger, Lou Ferrigno, LUCKY, Macallan, Marlboro, Napa Valley College, NYU/New York University, Plymouth Road Runner, RC Cola, Ritz Carlton Hotels, Rockefeller Center, Rod Sterling, Saturday Night Fever, Select Model Management, Sergio Rossi, Statue of Liberty, Stoli (Stolichnaya), Sweet & Low Yogurt, TaB Cola, Tiffany Jewelers, Times Square, Tra Vigne, Twilight Zone, Visine, *Vogue Magazine*, Waldorf, Walkman, Wall Street Journal, War Memorial Opera House, Yale University, Zenith TV, Zsa-Zsa Gabor

CPSIA information can be obtained at www.ICGtesting.com
Printed in the USA
LVOW08s2309290616

494621LV00001B/127/P